CW00523625

H. Irving Hancock

The Grammar School Boys of Gridley

H. Irving Hancock

The Grammar School Boys of Gridley

1st Edition | ISBN: 978-3-75237-037-9

Place of Publication: Frankfurt am Main, Germany

Year of Publication: 2020

Outlook Verlag GmbH, Germany.

The Grammar School Boys of Gridley

By

H. IRVING HANCOCK

CHAPTER I

"OLD DUT" TELLS A STORY—DICK ANOTHER——

"Master Prescott, what are you doing?"

The voice of Mr. E. Dutton Jones rasped out rather sharply, jarring on the generally studious air of the eighth-grade room of the Central Grammar School.

"What were you doing, Master Prescott?" repeated the stern voice of the principal.

Dick Prescott had glanced up, somewhat startled and confused. By this time every boy's and girl's eyes had turned away from text-books toward Dick Prescott.

"I was whispering, sir," confessed Dick.

"Oh, was that all?" demanded the somewhat ironical voice of Mr. E. Dutton Jones, more commonly known as "Old Dut."

"Yes, sir."

"To whom were you whispering?"

"To Master Hazelton."

"If I am intruding on no confidences, what were you whispering about?" continued Old Dut.

"I——" began Dick, and then his face turned still more red under the curious gaze of some fifty boys and girls. "I was telling Master Hazelton a funny story."

"Do you think it was very funny?" inquired Old Dut.

"The story? Yes, sir."

The broad grin that promptly spread over Harry Hazelton's face seemed to confirm Dick's claim as to the humorous quality of the story.

"Master Prescott," adjudged the principal, "you may rise in your seat and tell the story to the whole class, myself included. On this dull, rainy day I feel certain that we all need a good laugh."

A smile that grew to a titter in some quarters of the room greeted Dick as he struggled half-shamefacedly to his feet.

"Go on with the story," encouraged Old Dut. "Or, rather, begin at the beginning. That's the right way to serve up a story."

"I—I'd rather not tell the story, sir," protested young Prescott.

"Why not?" demanded the principal sharply.

"Well, because, sir—I'd rather not. That's all."

Principal Jones frequently employed that grilling way of questioning one of his pupils, and his implied sarcasm had a very effective way of making young offenders squirm before the class.

Whispering, in itself, is not a criminal offense, yet it often has a sad effect on the discipline of a schoolroom, and of late Old Dut had been much annoyed by whisperers.

"So you won't tell us all that choice story, eh, Master Prescott?" insisted the principal, half coaxingly.

"On account of its being such a very personal one I'd rather not, sir," Dick answered, still standing by his desk. "I might hurt some one's feelings."

"Too bad!" murmured Old Dut. "And just after we had all been enlivened by the hope of hearing something really funny! I know your rare quality of humor, Master Prescott, and I had promised myself a treat. My own disappointment in the matter may be cured, but what about the boys and girls of this class? I know that they are all still eager to hear a really funny story."

Old Dut paused, glancing impressively about the room. Dick, shifting first to one foot and then to the other, had not yet succeeded in parting with much of the fiery color that had flamed up to his cheeks, temples and forehead.

"Master Prescott," announced the principal, "the class shall not be deprived of its expected treat. I will tell a story, and I think you will find some of the elements of humor in it. Will you kindly step this way?"

Dick went forward, head up and chest thrown out, a look almost of defiance in his clear, blue eyes as a titter ran around the room.

"Stand right here beside me," coaxed Old Dut. "Now, let me see if I can remember the story. Yes; I believe I can. It runs something like this."

Then Old Dut began his story. It was a very ordinary one that had to do with a boy's disobedience of his father's commands. But it had a "woodshed" end to it.

"So," continued Old Dut, "Johnson took his boy out to the shed. There, with a sigh as though his heart were breaking, the old man seated himself on the chopping block. He gathered his son across his knee—about like this."

Here Principal Jones suddenly caught Dick Prescott and brought that lad across his own knee. The expectant class now tittered loudly.

"I can't tell this story unless I have quiet," announced Old Dut, glancing up and around the room with a reproachful look.

Then, after clearing his throat, the principal resumed:

"'Johnny,' said the old man huskily, 'I know what my duty in the matter really is. I ought to give you a good spanking, like this (*whack!*). But I haven't the heart to give you such a blow as you deserve. (Whack!) But the next time (whack!), I'm going to give you (whack!) just such a good one (whack! whack!) as you deserve. (Whack! whack!) So, remember, Johnny (whack!), and don't let me catch you (whack!) disobeying me again. (Whack! whack!)."

Each "whack" Old Dut emphasized by bringing down his own broad right hand on Dick's unprotected body.

A few flashing eyes there were in the young audience, and a few sympathetic glances from the girls, but, for the most part, the class was now in a loud roar of laughter.

"That's the story," announced Old Dut, gently restoring Dick Prescott to his feet. "I think you all see the point to it. Perhaps there's a moral to it, also. I really don't know."

Pallor due to a sense of outraged dignity now struggled for a place in the red that covered Dick Prescott's face.

"You may go to your seat, Master Prescott."

Dick marched there, without a glance backward.

"Now, that we've had our little indulgence in humor," announced Old Dut dryly, "we will all return to our studies."

There was silence again in the room, during which the rain outside began to come down in a flood.

"I'll get the fellows to-night—for that—and we'll carry Old Dut's front gate off and throw it in the river!" ran vengefully through Dave Darrin's mind.

"Old Dut needn't look for his late posies to bloom until the frost comes this year," reflected Greg Holmes, while he pored, apparently, over the many-colored map of Asia. "I'll get some of the fellows out to-night, and we'll make a wreck scene in Old Dut's flower beds."

Dick said nothing, even to himself, as he picked up his much-thumbed book on physiology and turned the pages. He was smarting not only from the indignity to which he had been treated, but quite as much from the masterful way in which Old Dut had punctuated that "funny story" with his broad right hand.

Once in a while Old Dut cast a sly glance in Dick's direction.

"That young man will bear watching," mused the principal, as he caught a sudden flash in Prescott's eye, as the latter glanced up.

The recitation in arithmetic soon came along. This was one of Dick's favorite studies, and, wholly forgetting his late experience, so it seemed, he covered himself with glory in his blackboard demonstration of an intricate problem in interest and discount.

Then the class settled down to twenty minutes' more study.

"Master Prescott," broke in Old Dut's voice, at last, "did you think my story a funny one?"

"Pretty fair, sir," answered Dick, looking up and straight into the eyes of the principal.

"Only 'pretty fair,' eh? Could you tell me a funnier story?"

"I'm pretty sure I could, yes, sir," answered Dick, with great promptness. "Only—*I don't believe I'm big enough yet!*"

There was a moment's hush. Then the class caught the spirit of the answer. A few titters sounded, cautiously—to be followed instantly by an explosion of laughter. Even Old Dut had to join in the laugh.

"That young man will bear watching," thought the principal grimly. "He's my best pupil, and one of the most mischievous. I'd rather have any youngster mischievous than stupid."

Glancing at the clock, Principal Jones swung around, running a finger down a line of push buttons in the wall back of his seat. In this fashion did he announce to the schoolrooms of the seven lower grades that morning recess time had come. Then he swung back.

"Attention, class!" he called. Tap! sounded a bell. The eighth-grade boys and girls rose, standing by their seats.

Tap! At the second bell the lines filed out in orderly fashion to the coatrooms, at the sides of the schoolroom.

But many of the young people soon came back. It was raining heavily outdoors on this September morning. True, the boys' and girls' basements served as playrooms in bad weather, but the basements were always crowded at such times, and many of the young people preferred to pass the recess time in the schoolroom.

"Old Dut's getting rather too fresh these days," growled Greg Holmes to his chum. Then whispered in Dick's ear:

"We'll get hunk with him to-night. Some of us will go around and play the wreck scene in his flower gardens."

"Nothing doing," retorted Dick briefly.

"I know a good one," whispered Dave Darrin, his dark eyes flashing with anticipated mischief. "We'll switch Old Dut's new gate off and play Moses in the bulrushes at the river bank."

"Say," demanded Dick, gazing curiously at his tempters, "since when have you thought I don't know enough to pay back my own grudges!"

"Have you got a scheme?" demanded Tom Reade eagerly, while Harry Hazelton and Dan Dalzell, sure that Dick had a "corker" of a scheme, grinned as happily as though they had already seen it put through with a rush.

"Have you got a scheme?" insisted Dave.

"Maybe," replied Dick evasively.

"Any of you fellows going down to the basement?" asked Hazelton after a moment.

"What's the use?" questioned Dick. "Tramp down three flights of stairs, and then climb the flights again in ten minutes."

With that Dick sauntered into the schoolroom. Old Dut was seated at his desk, a half dozen of the girls standing about, eating apples or candy, and talking with the principal.

"Only girls over there by Prin's desk," thought Dick with some dissatisfaction. He wandered about for a few minutes, but at last went up to Old Dut's desk as though being reluctantly drawn there by some magnet.

"Get next," nudged Dave Darrin, poking Hazelton in the side. As Dave sauntered over to the desk Harry followed. Tom Reade seemed interested in the scene. Greg Holmes and Dan Dalzell strolled over, arm in arm.

Seeing such an invasion of boys, the girls gave back for a few feet, though they did not quit the scene.

"Funny the Detroits didn't win the championship this year, isn't it?" Dick asked innocently.

"The Detroits haven't any show," returned Darrin half disgustedly.

"They've got nearly a month to play yet, but the Detroits are no good this year."

"If all the Detroits were in a class with Pendleton, their new pitcher, this year," Dick contended, "the Detroits would show class enough."

Old Dut looked up with interest. A thoroughly skilled and capable teacher, he had always believed in encouraging sports and athletics.

"That Pendleton fellow is more than a wonder with a ball," Dick went on warmly. "I saw him pitch a game against the New Yorks this summer, and I dreamed about it for a week after."

"What's Pendleton's strong point?" followed up Dave Darrin.

"Everything in the pitching line," Dick answered.

"But what is his best point of all, Prescott?" broke in Old Dut.

Even that experienced school principal had tumbled into the trap that Dick Prescott had so ingeniously laid for him.

"Well, sir," replied Dick, wheeling around to the principal, every trace of resentment gone from his young face, "I should say that Pendleton's most noticeable trick is the way he twists and handles the ball when he's getting ready to drive in his curve. I watched Pendleton's work that day, and I think I stole the principle on which he uses his right wrist."

"Show me," unsuspiciously invited Old Dut.

Dick started to curve an imaginary ball in his right hand, then glanced over the principal's desk. A small, but thick, heavy book lay there.

"Well, I should say," Prescott resumed, "that Pendleton handles the ball about like this."

Picking up the book, Dick used both hands in trying to give it the right preliminary curve.

"But his delivery is, of course, the great feature," the lad went on. "When Pendleton has the ball curved just right, he raises his right and lets it go like this!"

Dick was facing the bevy of girls. They were so certain he was going to hurl the book in their direction that they scattered with little cries of alarm.

So forcefully had young Prescott prepared for the throw that the book did leave his hand, though the boy made a frantic effort—apparently—to recover the missile.

Not toward the retreating girls, however, did the book fly. It spun nearly at right angles, and——

Smack! it went, full into the face of Principal E. Dutton Jones.

"Oh, I beg your pardon, sir!" cried Dick in a voice ringing with remorse. "That must hurt you very much, sir."

"It is nothing," replied Old Dut gamely, though the unexpected shock had nearly taken his breath. Then he put one hand up to his injured face. "Why, I believe my nose is bleeding," he added, making a quick dive for his handkerchief.

In truth the nose was bleeding. Old Dut made a specialty of low-cut vests and white, immaculate shirt-fronts. Before the handkerchief was in place, three bright, crimson drops had fallen, rendering the shirt-front a gruesome sight to look at.

"Oh, sir, I hope you will excuse me," followed up Dick.

"Oh, yes; certainly," dryly returned the principal, as he rose and made for his private room. There was a handbowl in there, with hot and cold water, and the principal of the Central Grammar School of Gridley was soon busy repairing his personal appearance.

No sooner had he vanished behind the open door than Dave Darrin, Tom Reade, Dan Dalzell, Greg Holmes, Harry Hazelton and several other boys grinned broadly in their huge delight. Dick Prescott, however, admirable actor that he was, still wore a look of concern on his rather fine young face.

"One thing I've learned to-day, which I ought to have known before," grimly mused Old Dut, as he sopped a wet towel to his injured nose. "Dick Prescott doesn't need any guardian. He can look out for himself!"

"Wasn't it awful?" repeated a girl's voice out in the schoolroom.

"No," replied her companion. "I don't think it was. After what he did it served him just right!"

"I'm getting the usual sympathy that is awarded to the vanquished," smiled Old Dut to himself. "That's Laura Bentley's voice. She didn't laugh when I was having my innings with Dick. She flushed up and looked indignant."

Before Old Dut felt that he was in shape to present himself, all of the eight grades had received seven minutes' additional recess.

At last studies were resumed. Old Dut, however, noted that whenever one of the boys or girls looked up and caught sight of his expansive, crimsoned shirt-front, a smile always followed.

CHAPTER II

A BRUSH ON THE STREET

By the time that the noon dismissal bell rang the rain had ceased, and the sun was struggling out.

Out in the coatroom Dick snatched his hat from the nail as though he were in haste to get away.

"I'll race you home, as far as we go together," proposed Dave Darrin.

"Go you!" hovered on the tip of Prescott's tongue, but just then another thought popped into Dick's mind. It was a manly idea, and he had learned to act promptly on such impulses.

"Wait a moment," he answered Darrin. "I've got something to do."

With that Dick marched back into the schoolroom. Old Dut, looking up from the books that he was placing in a tidy pile on the platform desk, smiled.

"I came back to ask, sir, if your nose pains?"

Old Dut shot a keen glance at young Prescott, for long experience had taught the school-teacher that malice sometimes lurks behind the most innocent question from a boy. Then he answered:

"I'm glad to be able to report, Master Prescott, that my nose is causing me no trouble whatever."

"I'm very glad of that, sir. I've been a bit uncomfortable, since recess, thinking that perhaps my—that my act had broken your nose, and that you were just too game to let any one know. I'm glad no real harm was done, sir."

Then Dick turned, anxious to get out into the open as quickly as possible.

"One moment, Master Prescott!"

Dick wheeled about again.

"Are you sure that the book-throwing was an accident?"

"I—I am afraid it wasn't, sir," Dick confessed, reddening.

"Then, if you threw the book into my face on purpose, why did you do it!"

"I was a good deal provoked, Mr. Jones."

"Oh! Provoked over the funny story that I told you this forenoon?"

"Not over the story, sir; but your manner of telling it."

Old Dut had hard work to keep back the smile that struggled for an appearance on his face.

"Revenge, was it, Master Prescott?"

"Well, I felt that it was due me, Mr. Jones, to get even for the show that you made of me before the class."

"Master Prescott, we won't go into the details of whether I was justified in illustrating my story this morning in the manner that I did, or whether you were right in coming back at me after the fashion that you did. But I am going to offer one thought for your consideration. It is this—that the man who devotes too much thought to 'getting even' with other folks is likely to let slip a lot of good, solid chances for getting ahead in the world. I don't blame any fellow for protecting his own rights and dignity, but just think over what I said, won't you, about the chap who spends too much of his time thinking up ways to get even with others?"

"There's a good idea in that, sir," Dick assented.

"Of course you've heard, Master Prescott, that 'revenge is sweet?'"

"Yes; I have."

"And I believe, Master Prescott, that the saying is often true. But did it ever strike you, in this connection, that sweet things often make one sick at his stomach? I believe this is just as true of revenge as it is of other sweets. And now run along, or you won't have time to do justice to the pudding that your mother has undoubtedly been baking for you this morning."

As Dick hastened from the room he found Dave Darrin waiting for him. Out in the corridor beyond these two encountered Holmes, Dalzell, Hazelton and Reade, for these six boys of the "top grade" generally stuck together in all things concerning school life.

"Was Old Dut blowing you up for showing him how to pitch a book?" inquired Greg.

"No; Old Dut doesn't seem to hold that in for me very hard," smiled Prescott. "But he was giving me something to think over."

"Huh!" muttered Greg, as the boys walked down the outer steps. "I'd like to give him something to think about. Why did you get so crusty when I sprang the idea of doing the wreck scene in his flower beds to-night?"

"Because the idea was too kiddish," returned Dick. "Besides, Old Dut was talking to me a good deal along such lines."

"Did you go and tell him what I wanted to do?" flared Greg.

"I didn't. But Old Dut pinned me down and asked me whether that book throwing were really an accident, and I had to admit that it wasn't. Now, listen!"

Dick thereupon repeated his conversation with Principal Jones.

"He's a wise man, all right," nodded Harry Hazelton.

"I guess so," nodded Dave Darrin. "After all, it would look rather kiddish in us to go slipping up to his front yard in the dark night, lifting off his front gate and carrying it down to the river."

"It would be stealing, or wasting, property, also," agreed Tom Reade.

"So, fellows," resumed Dick, "I guess——"

"Hullo! What's going on down there?" broke in Darrin hastily, as all six of the Grammar School boys looked ahead.

A woman's scream had caught their ear.

"It's Mrs. Dexter," muttered Hazelton.

"And that rascally husband of hers," added Greg Holmes.

"Some new row, of course," broke in Dan Dalzell.

"It's a shame!" burst from Dick.

"That Dexter fellow ought to be hung," growled Tom Reade. "He's always bothering that woman, and she's one of the nicest ever. But now he won't let her alone, just because her grandfather had to die and leave Mrs. Dexter a lot of money."

The little city of Gridley was quite familiar with the domestic troubles of the Dexters. The woman was young and pretty, and good-hearted. Abner Dexter, on the other hand, was good-looking and shiftless. He had married Jennie Bolton because he believed her family to be wealthy, and Dexter considered himself too choice for work. But the Bolton money had all belonged to the grandfather, who, a keen judge of human nature, had guessed rightly the nature of Abner Dexter and had refused to let him have any money.

Dexter had left his wife and little daughter some two years before the opening of this story. Three months before old man Bolton had died, leaving several hundred thousand dollars to Mrs. Dexter. Then Dexter had promptly reappeared. But Mrs. Dexter no longer wanted this shiftless, extravagant man about, and had told him so plainly. Dexter had threatened to make trouble, and the wife had thereupon gone to court and had herself appointed sole guardian of her little daughter. At the same time she had turned some money over to her husband—common report said ten thousand dollars—on his promise to go away and not bother her again.

Plainly he had not kept his word. As Dick and his chums glanced down the quiet side street they saw husband and wife standing facing each other. The man was scowling, the woman half-tearful, half-defiant. Behind her, in her left hand, Mrs. Dexter held a small handbag.

"I'd like to be big enough to be able to enjoy the pleasure of thrashing a fellow like that Dexter!" growled Dave Darrin, his eyes flashing.

"There's a man standing a little way below the pair," announced Dick. "I wonder what he's doing, for he seems to be watching the couple intently. I hope he's on Mrs. Dexter's side."

Unconsciously Dick and his friends had halted to watch the proceedings ahead of them.

"No, I won't," replied Mrs. Dexter sharply, to something that her husband had said.

Abner Dexter talked rapidly, a black scowl on his face meanwhile.

"No, you won't! You don't dare!" replied the woman, her voice sounding as though she had summoned all her courage by an effort.

Dexter suddenly sprang closer to the woman. The next instant both were struggling for possession of the little black bag that she carried.

"Stop!" cried Mrs. Dexter desperately. "Help! He-lp!"

"Fellows, I don't know that we're bound to stand for that," muttered Dick Prescott quickly. "She's calling for help. Come along."

Dick was off down the street like a streak, the others following, though Dave was closest to his chum.

"Here, what are you doing, mister?" demanded Dick, as he darted up to where the pair were struggling.

Dexter would have had the bag in his own possession by this time, had he not turned to see what the onrush of boys meant.

"None of your business what I'm doing," he replied savagely. "You schoolboys run along out of this."

"Don't go! Help me," pleaded the woman. "He's trying to rob me!"

"You boys clear out, or it will be worse for you!" growled Dexter.

"The lady wins!" Dick announced coolly, though he was shaking somewhat from excitement. "You let go of her and her property."

But Dexter, his face black with scowls, still clutched tightly with his right hand at the little handbag, to which Mrs. Dexter was clinging with both her hands.

"You let go of that bag," challenged Dick, "or six of us will sail into you. I think we can handle you. We'll try, anyway."

"Yes; make him let go," begged Mrs. Dexter. "I have money and jewels here, and he is trying to take them away from me."

"Going to do as the lady wishes?" inquired Dick, stepping closer.

Abner Dexter shot another angry glare at the sextette of Grammar School boys. They were closing in around him, and it looked as though they meant business.

"Gus!" called Dexter sharply.

The man who had been standing a short distance away now ran up to the spot.

"Hullo, what do you want!" asked Dick coolly. "Are you the understudy in this game of robbery?"

"I'm an officer," retorted the fellow sharply.

"Secretary to some Chinese laundry company, eh?" jeered Dick.

"I'm a police officer," retorted the man sharply, at the same time displaying a shield.

That put a different look on matters with some of young Prescott's friends. Dick, however, was a boy not easily daunted.

"If you're an officer," he inquired, "why don't you get busy and do your duty? Here's a man trying to rob his wife, just because she happens to have more money than he has."

"A man can't legally steal from his wife, nor a woman from her husband," retorted the policeman bullyingly. "There is no crime being committed here. But if you boys try to interfere you'll be disturbing the peace, and I'll run you all in."

Mrs. Dexter looked bewildered and frightened. She even let go of the handbag with one hand. Dick saw this, and quickly broke in:

"Mrs. Dexter, don't you let Mr. Dexter have that handbag unless you want to do it. We'll stand by you."

"Oh, will you?" glared the policeman. "You boys run along, or I'll gather you all in."

"Where are you a policeman?" inquired Dick Prescott, eyeing the fellow with interest. "You're not a Gridley officer, for I know every one of them."

"Never you mind where I'm from," jeered the man harshly. "I'm a policeman. That'll have to be enough for you youngsters. If you don't trot fast down the street I'll gather you in."

Some of Dick's chums were now inclined to feel that they had broken in at the wrong place, but not so their young leader.

"You haven't any right to make arrests in Gridley," retorted Dick defiantly. "And, even if you had, you couldn't stop us from defending a woman. Tom, you and Greg stand by me. Dave, you lead the rest. We'll make Dexter let go of his wife's property and let her alone. If this man who says he's an officer interferes, Greg, Tom and I will devote our attention to him!"

"Great!" snarled Dexter jeeringly. "You're all young jailbirds!"

"Are you going to let go of Mrs. Dexter's property?" challenged Dick.

"I'm not."

"Come on, fellows—let's sail into him."

Dick was an able general, having his small force under good discipline. There was a sudden rush of boys. True, they averaged only thirteen years of age, but there were six of them, and they were determined.

Dexter let go of the handbag in a hurry. He had to do so, in order to defend himself.

At the same moment the man named as "Gus" jumped into the fray.

"Three to each man!" yelled Dick, and thus the force was divided.

The self-styled policeman reached out with the flat of his hand, knocking Greg Holmes off his feet. But, as he did so, Dick dropped down in front of the man, wrapping both arms around the fellow's knees. Then Dick rose. It required the exertion of all his strength, but he succeeded in toppling Gus over onto his back.

At the same time Abner Dexter was having all he could do, for three very determined schoolboys were assailing him. At last Dexter turned to retreat, but Dan Dalzell thrust a foot before him and tripped him.

"All down!" yelled Dan. "Set 'em up in the other alley!"

Though downed for the moment, the two men were disposed to make a livelier fight of it than ever. It was a brisk, picturesque, rough-and-tumble fight that followed, in which the young boys got a deal of rough handling.

Frightened, yet fascinated, Mrs. Dexter tottered against the fence and stood looking on.

Things might yet have fared badly with Dick and his friends had not a newcomer arrived on the scene. He came running, and proved to be Policeman Whalen in uniform.

"Here! What's on?" demanded the Gridley officer. "Let up on kicking them boys! I want you!"

With that Whalen, who was a big and powerful man, grabbed Abner Dexter by the coat collar and pulled him to his feet. With this prisoner in tow, he moved up and seized Gus in similar fashion.

"Now, what's the row?" demanded Officer Whalen.

"Arrest these boys for assault!" quivered Dexter in a passion.

"Yes, arrest them!" insisted Gus. "I'm an officer, too, and I was trying to take them in."

"You didn't seem to be having very good luck at it," grinned Whalen. "But I know these boys, and they're all good lads."

"Arrest them, just the same! They were assaulting me," insisted Dexter angrily.

"And what were you doing?" insisted Whalen wonderingly.

"He was trying to steal jewels and money from his wife," interposed Dick Prescott.

"Bah!" growled Dexter. "A man can't steal from his wife."

"But he can assault her," returned Policeman Whalen. "And a man can disturb the peace with his wife, just as handily as he can anywhere else. Mrs. Dexter, are these lads telling the truth?"

"Oh, yes, officer! My husband was trying to take this satchel away from me, and he knew that it contains my jewels and thirty-five hundred dollars in cash."

"Do you want him arrested?"

"Yes; I—I'm afraid I shall have to have him arrested, or he'll go right on annoying me."

"Will you appear against him, Mrs. Dexter?"

"Yes."

"Then I'll take him along. And what about this fellow?"

"Me?" demanded Gus with offended dignity. "I'm a police officer."

"What's your name?"

"August Driggs."

"Where are you a policeman?"

"In Templeton."

"Why were you lads fighting Officer Driggs?" inquired Whalen blandly.

Dick supplied some of the details, Dave others. Mrs. Dexter confirmed the statements that they made.

"I guess I'll take you along, too, Driggs," announced Policeman Whalen.

"But I'm a police officer!" protested Driggs aghast.

"Police officers can be arrested like anyone else, when they break the law," announced Policeman Whalen dryly. "Come along, the two of you! Mrs. Dexter, you wouldn't like to be seen walking along with us, but I'll ask you to be at the station house inside of five minutes."

"I'll be there, officer," promised the woman.

"Do you want us, too?" inquired Dick. He and all of his friends were eager to see the affair through to the finish.

"No; I know where to find you lads, if you're wanted," grinned Policeman Whalen. "I don't want a big crowd following. Mrs. Dexter, ma'am, I'll be looking for you to be on hand sharp."

With that the broad-backed policeman started off with two savage prisoners in tow.

"Say, if we're to have any dinner and get back to school on time, we'll have to be moving fast," declared Dan Dalzell.

"I thought we were surely going to get into a lot of trouble," muttered Hazelton, as the youngsters moved along rapidly. "But Whalen knew his business."

"I hope the judge can send that Dexter fellow up for a good, long time," muttered Dick. "He's been annoying that poor woman all the time lately."

"Just because she has her grandfather's money at last," grumbled Dave Darrin.

Soon the youngsters came to a point where they had to separate. But all hands were back at school on time. The work of the afternoon was duly progressing when the telephone bell at the principal's desk rang.

Old Dut held what proved to be a mysterious conversation for a few moments. Then he wound up with:

"All right. I'll send them right over."

Ringing off, Old Dut glanced atDick.

"Master Prescott, it appears that you, Darrin, Reade, Holmes, Dalzell and Hazelton saw some trouble on the street this noon."

"Yes, sir."

"All six of you are wanted, at once, down at court, to give evidence. You are excused. If you get through at court early enough, come back to finish your afternoon's work."

Six Grammar School boys rose and filed out quietly. How enviously the other boys in the room stared after them! How curiously the girls glanced at the young heroes who were now wanted on the government's business!

"Say," ventured Dan as soon as they got outside, "I hope the judge orders Dexter hanged."

"He'll hardly do that," retorted Dave. "A street row is hardly a hanging offense. If it were, there'd be a lot of fellows missing from the Central Grammar School."

"So we're called in to help decide the case?" asked Greg, puffing up.

"Oh, get busy with some brains!" scoffed Dick airily. "We haven't anything to do with deciding the case. That's what the judge is paid for. But we're wanted just to tell what we know. Say, you fellows, be careful you don't get so rattled that you try to tell a lot of things that you don't know."

In due time they reached the court building. Grown suddenly very quiet and almost scared, these six thirteen-year-old boys filed upstairs. A policeman stood before the door of the courtroom.

"May we go in?" whispered Dick.

"Of course," nodded the policeman. "Take your hats off."

The officer conducted the sextette of young witnesses inside, past a group or two of loungers who made up the usual police-court audience, and thence on before the bench.

At one side, at this end of the room, sat Dexter and Driggs. Right in front of the clerk of the court were seated Mrs. Dexter and a lawyer. Officer Whalen lounged near the two prisoners.

"These are the lads, your honor," nodded Policeman Whalen, after giving Dick & Co. a keen looking over.

"Swear them, Mr. Clerk," said the Justice.

Solemnly the six youngsters held up their right hands and took the oath. Then Justice Lee began to question them. From Dick, first, he drew out the story of the dispute in the street. Then the others told the same story.

"Why did you boys interfere?" asked the justice of Prescott.

"Because, sir," Dick answered, "we didn't want to see a woman ill-treated on the street."

"A very good reason," nodded Justice Lee approvingly. "But weren't you afraid of Driggs, here, who is really a police officer?"

"No, sir; I didn't believe that a police officer had any more right than any one else to break the law."

"You boys have acted very sensibly," nodded Justice Lee. "Dexter, do you wish to question any of these young witnesses?"

Dexter shook his head, scowling.

"Do you, Driggs?"

"No, your honor. 'Twouldn't be any use."

"You're right about that, I imagine," nodded the justice. "Boys, the court wishes to express its pleasure over your good sense, and to praise you for your chivalry and courage. You did just right—as the court hopes you will always do under similar circumstances. Dexter, stand up. Driggs, also."

The two prisoners arose, sullen enough in their appearance.

"Dexter, you have been guilty of disturbing the peace. I do not believe a mere fine sufficient in your case. I therefore sentence you to serve thirty days in jail. Driggs, your primary offense was about as great as Dexter's, but your offense is worse, for you are a police officer, and you tried to throw the strength of your position around the acts of the prisoner. The court therefore sentences you to sixty days in jail."

"We both wish to appeal, your honor," cried Dexter, his face aflame.

"Dexter's bail will then be fixed at two hundred dollars; Driggs's at four hundred dollars. Are you prepared to furnish bail?"

"I will furnish the cash for both of us," announced Abner Dexter, drawing a roll of banknotes from a pocket.

Mrs. Dexter and her lawyer filed out while this matter was being arranged with the clerk of the court. Dick and his friends, at a sign from the court, left the room as soon as they had received their fees as witnesses.

"So he pays the money, Dexter does, and walks out?" grunted Dan Dalzell.

"Oh, no," Dick answered. "Dexter and his friend have to be tried over again in a higher court. That money is just their forfeit in case they don't show up for trial."

"They won't," predicted Greg.

"I don't know," murmured Dick. "Six hundred dollars would be a lot of money to lose."

By hastening, the Grammar School boys were back in school for the last hour of the session.

CHAPTER III

FOOTBALL—WITHOUT RULES

School was out for the day. Three quarters of the boys belonging to the four upper grades made a bee line for a field about a block away. The magnet was a football that Dave Darrin proudly carried tucked under his left arm.

"I wanter play!"

"Let me try just one good kick with it, Dave!"

"Take a stroll," advised Darrin laconically. "How can I blow up the ball and talk to you fellows, too?"

"Hurry up, then. We want to give the ball a fierce old kick."

"No kids in this," announced Dave, rather loftily. "Only fellows in the eighth and seventh grades. Fellows in the grades below the seventh are only kids and would get hurt."

"Oh, say!"

"That isn't fair!"

The protests were many and vigorous from sixth and fifth-grade boys, but Darrin, ignoring them all, went placidly on inflating the pigskin. At last the task was completed.

"Hurrah! Now, Dave, give it a boost and let us all have some fun!" cried the boys. But Darrin coolly tucked the ball under one arm.

"Dick Prescott has a few remarks to make first," Dave announced.

"Dick going to make a speech?"

"Cut it, and start the ball moving!"

"Won't you fellows interrupt your music lessons long enough to listen to an idea that some of us have been talking over?" called Dick. "Now, fellows, you know this is the time when the crack Gridley High School football team is hard at work. We're all proud of the Gridley High School eleven. A lot of you fellows expect to go to High School, and I know you'd all like a chance to play on Gridley High's eleven."

"Set the ball moving!"

"Wait a minute," Dick insisted. "Now, fellows, no Grammar School in

Gridley has ever had an eleven."

"How could we," came a discontented wail, "if we have to stand here and see Dave just do nothing but hold the ball?"

"Fellows," Dick went on impressively, "it's time to have Grammar School football teams here in Gridley. Central Grammar ought to have one, North Grammar one and South Grammar one. Then our three Grammar Schools could play a championship series among themselves."

"Hooray! Give the ball a throw, Dave!"

"So, fellows," Dick continued, "a lot of us think we ought to organize a football team at once. Then we can challenge North Grammar and South Grammar. We can practise the rest of this month, and next month we can play off our games. What do you say?"

"Hooray!"

"We'll have two teams," called Dave. "We'll call one team the Rangers and the other the Rustlers. Now, let's make Dick captain of the Rangers."

"All right!"

"And Tom Craig captain of the Rustlers."

"Good!"

"All right, then," nodded Dave. "Dick, you pick out the Rangers; Craig, you go ahead with the Rustlers. After we've practised a few times we'll pick the best men from both elevens, and make up the Central Grammar eleven. Get busy, captains!"

Forthwith the choosing began. Dick chose all his chums for his own eleven. And no boy lower than seventh grade was allowed on either team.

"Now, who'll be referee?" demanded Dick. "Captain Craig, have you any choice?"

"Have we got any fellows, not on either team, who really know the rules?" asked Tom Craig dubiously.

There was a hush, for this was surely a stumbling block. It seemed clear that a referee ought to know the rules of the game.

"What's up, kids?" called a friendly voice.

The speaker was Len Spencer, a young man who had been graduated from the High School the June before, and who was now serving his apprenticeship as reporter on one of the two local daily papers, the morning "Blade."

"Oh, see here, Len!" called Dick joyously. "You're just the right fellow for us. You know the football rules?"

"I have a speaking acquaintance with 'em," laughed Len.

Dick rapidly outlined what was being planned, adding:

"You can put that in the 'Blade' to-morrow morning, Len, and state our challenge to North and South Grammars. Won't you?"

"Surely."

"But we want to practise this afternoon," Dick continued earnestly, "and we haven't any referee. Len, can't you spare us a little time? Won't you boss the first practice for us?"

"All right," agreed Len, after a little thought. "I'll tackle it for a while. Have you got your teams picked?"

"Teams all picked, and the ball ready. We'll have to place stones for goal posts, though."

"Hustle and do it, then," commanded Len. "I can't stay here forever."

Five minutes later the field was as ready as it could be made.

"Captains will now attend the toss-up," ordered Len Spencer, producing a coin from one of his pockets. "Heads for Craig, tails for Prescott."

It fell head up, and Craig chose his goal, and also the first kick-off.

Dick had been busily engaged in making up his line and backfield. There was some delay while Tom Craig accomplished this same thing.

"Now, one thing that all you youngsters want to remember," declared Len, "is that no player can play off-side. All ready?"

Both young football captains called out that they were. Len had provided himself with a pocket whistle loaned by one of the fifth-grade boys.

Trill-ll! Tom Craig kicked the ball himself, but it was a poor kick. The pigskin soon struck the ground.

"I'll try that over again," announced Tom.

But Dick and his own fighting line had already started. Dick, at center, with Dave on his right hand and Greg Holmes on his left, snatched up the ball and started with it for the Rustlers' goal.

A bunch of Rustlers opposed and tackled Prescott. Dick succeeded, by the help of Dave and Greg, in breaking through the line, but the Rustlers turned and were after him. Down went Dick, but he had the pigskin under him.

"Take it away from him, fellows!" panted Craig. But Len blew his whistle, following up the signal by some sharp commands that brought the struggle to a close.

"Prescott's side have the ball," declared Len, "and will now play off a snap-back. And, boys, one thing I must emphasize. I've told you that under the rules no man may play off-side. So, hereafter, if I find any of you off-side, I'm going to penalize that eleven."

Dick was whispering to some of his players, for, without any code of signals, he must thus instruct his fellows in the play that was to be made with the ball.

Then the whistle sounded. The Rangers put the ball through the Rustlers' line, and onward for some fifteen yards before the ball was once more down.

"Good work, Prescott," nodded Len Spencer. "Now, pass your orders for the next play, then hustle into line and snap-back."

Len placed the whistle between his lips and was about to blow it when Dave Darrin darted forward, holding up one hand.

"What's the trouble?" asked Len.

"Mr. Referee, count the men on the other team."

"Fifteen players," summed up Len. "That's too many. Captain Craig, you'll have to shed four men."

"Oh, let him have 'em all," begged Dick serenely. "Craig'll need 'em all to keep us from breaking through with the ball."

At blast of the whistle the pigskin was promptly in play again, both teams starting in with Indian yells. There was plenty of enthusiasm, but little or no skill. The thing became so mixed up that Len ran closer.

A human heap formed. Greg Holmes was somewhere down near the bottom of that mix-up, holding on to the ball for all he was worth. Over him sprawled struggling Rangers and fighting Rustlers. Other players, from both teams, darted forward, hurling themselves onto the heap with immense enthusiasm.

"The ball is down," remarked one eager young spectator disgustedly. "Len oughter blow his whistle."

"Yes, where's the whistle?" demanded other close-by spectators.

From somewhere away down toward the bottom of the heap came Len Spencer's muffled remark:

"I'll blow the whistle all right, if half a hundred of you Indians will get off my face for a minute!"

"Come out of that tangle, all of you," ordered Tom Craig, after pulling himself out of the squirming heap of boys. "It's against the rules to smother the referee to death. He has to be killed painlessly."

When the tangle had been straightened out Greg Holmes was found to be still doubled up, holding doggedly to the pigskin that had been his to guard.

"Get ready for the next snap-back," ordered Captain Dick.

"Don't do anything of the sort," countermanded Len. "I can see that what you youngsters need more than play, just at present, is a working knowledge of the rules. So listen, and I'll introduce you to a few principles of the game."

After ten minutes of earnest talk Len Spencer allowed the ball to be put once more in play.

At one time it was discovered that Craig, reinforced by enthusiastic onlookers from the sidelines, had seventeen men in his team. Dick, on the other hand, kept an alert eye to see that no more than eleven ranged up with his team.

"Now, that's enough for the first day," called out Len at last. "Neither side won, but the Rangers had by far the better of it. Now, before you fellows play to-morrow I advise you all to do some earnest studying of the rules of the game."

"Don't make too much fun of us in the 'Blade,' will you, Mr. Spencer?" begged Dick. "We really want to get a good Central Grammar eleven at work. We want to play the other Grammar Schools in town."

"Oh, no one but a fool could find it in his heart to make fun of boys who display as much earnestness as you youngsters showed to-day," Spencer replied soothingly.

"It's the first time we ever tried real play, you know," Dick went on.

"Yes; and you'll have to do a lot more practising before you can convince any one that you are doing any real playing," Len nodded. "Go after the rules. Memorize 'em. And watch the High School crowd play football. That will teach you a lot."

"I know we need it," Dick sighed. "But then, you see, Grammar School football is a brand-new thing."

"Why, now I come to think of it, I don't believe I ever did hear before of a Grammar School eleven," Len Spencer admitted.

At least twenty other boys followed Dick and his chums from the field on the way home.

"Say, Dick," called Tom Craig, "is the Central Grammar team going to have a uniform?"

"Why, I suppose we must have one," Dick answered.

"Where are we going to get the money?"

Dick looked blank at that. A football uniform costs at least a few dollars, and who ever heard of an average Grammar School boy having a few dollars, all his own to spend?

"I hadn't thought of that," muttered Prescott. "Oh, well, we'll have to find some way of getting uniforms. We've got to have 'em. That's all there is to it."

"'Where there's a will there's a way,'" quoted Tom Reade blithely.

But most of the fellows shook their heads.

"We can't get uniforms," declared several of the older eighth-grade boys.

"Then, if we can't we'll have to play without uniforms," Dick maintained. "We've got to play somehow. I hope you fellows won't go and lose your enthusiasm. Let's all hang together for football."

One by one the other boys dropped off, until only Dick and his five chums were left at a corner on Main Street.

"I'm afraid a lot of the fellows will go and let their enthusiasm cool over night," declared Harry Hazelton.

"Remember, fellows, we've got to have our football eleven, and we've got to keep at it until we can really play a good game," insisted Dick.

"But what if most all the fellows drop out?" demanded Dan Dalzell. "You know, that's the trouble with Grammar School fellows. They don't stick."

"There are six of us, and we'll all stick," proclaimed Dick. "That means that we've got to get only five other fellows to stick. Surely we can do that, if we've got hustle enough in us to play football at all."

"Oh, we'll have our eleven somehow," insisted Dave positively.

"How about our uniforms?" Tom Reade wanted to know.

"We'll have them, too," asserted Dick. "I don't know just how we'll do it, but we'll manage."

Dick Prescott and his chums were in much better spirits after that brief consultation. Then they separated, each going to his home for supper.

Dick's father and mother were proprietors of the most popular bookstore in Gridley. It stood on one of the side streets, just a little way down from Main Street. Over the store were the living rooms of the family. Dick was an only child.

After stowing away such an evening meal as only a healthy boy knows how to take care of, Dick reached for his cap.

"I'm going out to meet the fellows, mother, if you don't mind," said young Prescott.

"I'm sorry to say that there's just one matter that will delay you for perhaps twenty minutes," replied Mrs. Prescott. "Mrs. Davis was in and ordered some books this afternoon. She wants them delivered this evening, so I said I'd send you around with them. That won't bother you much, will it?"

"Not so much but that I'll get over it," laughed the boy. "Maybe I'll pick up one or two of the fellows, anyway."

"Richard, I'd rather you'd deliver the books before you meet any of your friends," urged Mrs. Prescott. "The books are worth about ten dollars, and if you have some of your friends along you may begin skylarking, and some of the books may get damaged."

"All right, mother. I'll go alone."

Off Dick started with the bundle, whistling blithely. All his thoughts were centered on the forming of the Central Grammar eleven, and that plan now looked like a winner.

"We won't let the High School fellows have all the fun," young Prescott mused as he hurried along.

He reached the rather large and handsome Davis house, rang the bell, delivered his books and then started back. His evening, up to nine o'clock, was now his own to do with as he pleased.

Suddenly the thought of the happenings at noon came back to his mind.

"What a mean fellow that Dexter is!" muttered the Grammar School boy. "I've heard folks say that Dexter is mean enough, and scoundrel enough, to kill his wife one of these days. Whew! I should think it would hurt to be so all-fired mean, and to have everyone despising you, as folks seem to despise Dexter. I hope the upper court will give him six months in jail, instead of one."

Prescott was moving along a dark street now. It bordered a broad field, back of which stood a deep grove. At the street end of the field was a neat, solid, stone wall.

Had Dick been looking ahead all the time he would have seen a man, coming down the street, start, take a swift look at the boy, and then dart behind a tree. But Prescott did not see until he reached the tree. Then the man stepped out.

"Prescott!" uttered Abner Dexter hoarsely, "I've been wanting to see you again!"

"That's more than I can say about you," retorted Dick, trying to edge away.

"No! You don't get away from me like that!" hissed Ab. Dexter sharply, twisting a hand on Dick's collar. Lifting the boy from his feet, Dexter hurled him over the wall into the field.

"Now, I'm going to settle with you, young meddler!" announced Dexter, vaulting the wall and throwing himself upon Dick. "When I get through with you you'll never feel like meddling with any one again!"

CHAPTER IV

AB. DEXTER'S TEMPER IS SQUALLY

"You're taking a lot upon yourself!" ventured Dick Prescott angrily.

"That's all right," laughed Dexter savagely. "Come along with me and I'll show you something really funny."

With that the man caught young Prescott up, starting across the field with him. Dick fought and struggled, but a grown man was too powerful for one thirteen-year-old boy.

"Don't make any noise," warned Dexter, as he ran with his "catch," "or I'll make you wish you hadn't opened your mouth!"

If he feared that Dick would call for help, this high-handed one was reckoning without a knowledge of the kind of boy he had to deal with. For Dick, though he was just a little more than slightly alarmed, would have been ashamed to call out for help.

"You think you're having a lot of fun," sputtered young Prescott angrily, "but you'll be sorry for this before you are through!"

"Through with whom?" demanded Dexter blandly, now.

"Before you're through with me. You'll find that you can't act like this around Gridley. Justice Lee will get hold of you again, first thing you know."

"Huh! I'll talk to you about that in a few minutes!"

"See here, where are you taking me?"

"Wherever I please."

"Then I don't know about that, either, Dexter. I've about made up my mind that I won't go any further with you."

"Oh, you won't, eh, boy! Well, just help yourself, if you can."

By this time Dexter had crossed the field and had run well inside of the grove.

Dick wriggled, getting one hand free—and then he struck Dexter a stinging blow in the face.

"Confound you!" growled the other. "I see that I've got to tame you, you young hornet!"

"You put me down, or I'll sting worse than a hornet," threatened Dick angrily. "I'm not a doormat that you can wipe your feet on."

"We'll see about that!" muttered Dexter, halting suddenly and throwing Dick savagely to the ground. He followed this up by sitting on the Grammar School boy.

Whack! Whack! Dexter struck him so savagely, both blows in the face, that Prescott gasped.

"I've got a few hundred more of those in reserve if you want 'em—or need 'em," Dick's captor advised him grimly. He still sat on the boy, looking down at him in the darkness with evil satisfaction.

"It doesn't take one long to find your number, Dexter," observed the boy undauntedly. "Your specialty is frightening women and pounding boys who offend you."

"Well, a lot of you boys hammered me this noon, didn't you!"

"Yes; and I wish I had a couple of the fellows here now," retorted Dick with spirit. "We'd soon make a coward like you seem small. You'd be on your knees, begging, if I had a couple of my chums here to help me."

"Well, you haven't got 'em, and I'll do all the talking that amounts to anything. Dick Prescott, you're the worst and freshest boy in Gridley!"

"Such a statement, coming from a fellow like you, amounts to high praise, Dexter," Dick retorted doughtily.

"None of your impudence, now, Dick Prescott! I've stood all the insolence from you that I'm going to allow."

"My! How big the man talks to the small boy!" taunted Dick. "And he had to drag the boy away off here, so that there wouldn't be a chance of another boy coming along. A man of your caliber, Dexter, may be brave enough to face one boy, when he's angry enough, but you wouldn't dare say 'boo' if one of my boy friends were here to back me up."

"I'll stop that sort of impudence right now," growled Dexter, stung more deeply by the taunts than he would have been willing to let the boy guess. "I'm pretty savage in my mind against you, at any rate, and I may as well let some of it out!"

Whack! smack! thump! Dexter began savagely to vent all of his bottled-up spite against young Prescott, striking him repeatedly, and with such force that the lad was soon aching all over.

Dick fought back as best he could, but, pinned down as he was, and in the grip of one three times as strong as himself, Dick could get in an effective blow only now and then. Such blows as he did land only served to fan Dexter's wrath to greater fury—and the boy suffered accordingly.

It would have been a brutal beating, under any circumstances, that Dick received. In his helpless condition it was doubly brutal.

"Now, do you think you've got enough to hold you for a while?" Ab. Dexter demanded, as he paused, panting.

"I'm just thinking about the time when you'll get it all back with interest!" snapped young Prescott.

"Oh, then you haven't hadenough—*yet*?"

"I had enough before you began."

"But you haven't learned to keep a civil tongue in your head?"

"Dexter," retorted the lad, speaking more earnestly than he was aware, "I try to keep not only a civil tongue, but a pleasant manner for every human being who tries to act decently. With you it's different. Before to-day I didn't know much about you. What little I did know wasn't to your credit. But now I know you to belong to nothing better than the scum of the earth. No human being with any self-respect could be decent with you!"

"You're getting worse than ever, are you?" sneered Dexter. "I see that my work is only half started."

With that Ab. Dexter threw himself upon the boy again, giving him an even more lively beating than before.

Dick Prescott, panting with his struggles, disdained to cry out, but saved all his strength to fight back.

At last, all but exhausted, Ab. Dexter paused.

"You got a little better lesson that time," boasted the wretch.

"And I got a small lunch while you were taking your dinner," retorted Prescott, no more daunted than before. "Your nose is bleeding and your lip is cut!"

"Yes, I know it! I'm going to take that out of you presently."

"Are you enjoying yourself, Dexter?" asked the boy tauntingly.

"Yes. And before I get through with you, I'm going to make sure that you'll never interfere in my affairs again."

"Do you mean that you expect I'll stand off the next time that I see you trying to frighten your wife into supporting a lazy loafer in style?" Dick asked dryly.

"Hang you! You haven't learned your lesson yet, have you?"

"If you're trying to make me 'respect' you, Dexter, you've acted the wrong way all through to-day. You're entitled to no more respect than an Indian would show a rattlesnake."

Ab. Dexter's face was ablaze with wrath. He had expected to make this Grammar School boy beg for mercy before things had gone half as far as they had. Dick Prescott's undaunted pluck bewildered the mean bully.

"I'll make you shut up, boy, before I'm through with you!" he warned the lad.

"There's just one way to do that, Dexter!"

"Eh?"

"You'll have to knock me out."

"I'll do that, then!"

It would be wrong to seek to give the reader an impression that young Prescott was not afraid, and did not mind his two thrashings. He was afraid that Dexter would go to great lengths, yet Dick would not give the bully satisfaction by admitting any fear.

"What you've got to do, before I get through with you," Dexter announced, "is to beg my pardon and to promise that you'll never again interfere with me."

"You'll wait a long while, then," jeered Dick, "and you'll get strong man's cramp in both arms!"

"And you've got to do more than promise that much," continued the bully. "You've got to promise, solemnly, to help me in some plans that I have for the future."

"Oh? Plans against your wife, I suppose."

"Very likely," half admitted Dexter. "Whatever the plans are, you're going to help me in them."

"You're going about in a fine way, Dexter, to get my cheerful help."

"Never mind about the cheerful part of it," snarled the man. "You're going to help me, and I'm going to tame you."

"Gracious! What a fine, large tail our cat is growing," laughed Dick, though his voice did not ring very mirthfully.

Dexter, still astride his young captive, raised his fist. Prescott did not flinch, and it suddenly struck the fellow that he was going about his business in the wrong way. Dexter had never looked for a young Grammar School boy to be so firm and undaunted.

"Now, don't be a fool, Prescott," he began, trying a new tack.

"You ought to be a fine teacher in the subject of good sense," suggested Dick mockingly.

"I think I can be."

"Fire away, then."

"Prescott, you don't have much spending money, do you?"

"Not enough to worry the bank with."

"You'd like more?"

"Of course."

"I'm going to find it for you."

"You are—or do you mean that your wife is?"

Ab. Dexter winked. He had not looked for the youngster to be so keen.

"Prescott, take it from an older man. It doesn't make so much difference, in this world, where the money comes from, if a fellow only has it."

"I guess, from your actions, that's about the way you feel about it, Dexter," rejoined the boy.

"Don't you feel the same way?"

"No; I'd like to be worth a million dollars, Dexter, but I don't believe I ever shall be."

"Why not?"

"Because the opportunities for getting a million honestly are not very plentiful, and I wouldn't have a dollar—or a million—with a stain on it!"

"You simpleton!" sneered Dexter.

"There are a few of us left in the world," Dick retorted complacently. "But you, Dexter, you wouldn't care whether it was money or slime, as long as you could spend it!"

"You're talking nonsense, boy," argued Dexter, restraining himself as best he could. "Now, see here, I'm sorry I thumped you. I've got a lot of use for a boy with as much sand and grit as you've shown. I can use you, and I can show you how to make a nice little lot of money by helping me in something that I have on hand. So come on. Get up and walk along with me while we talk it over."

Dexter rose, and Dick got to his feet as nimbly as he could. He ached, though, fortunately, he was not badly crippled by the pummeling that he had received.

"Come on, now, and let's take a little walk," urged the man persuasively.

But Dick Prescott glared back at the bully with all the contempt in the world in his look.

"Nothing doing in the way of walking together, Dexter," announced the boy.

"Why not?"

"Folks might see me with you."

"Suppose they did!"

"Then they'd imagine that I knew you. Dexter, a boy who hopes to grow up and become a useful citizen can't be too careful about the company he keeps."

"You confounded little imp! You're not tamed yet."

Dexter's foot struck against a stick lying on the ground. Snatching this weapon up and uttering a cry of rage, he sprang forward to fell the boy with the club.

CHAPTER V

FOOTBALL UNIFORMS IN SIGHT

Had Dick turned to run Ab. Dexter would have darted after him. The bully possessed much longer legs and prided himself on his speed.

To Dexter's amazement, however, Dick did not flinch or turn.

Perhaps there was not time enough. Again, perhaps young Prescott saw two other figures moving in the darkness.

At all events, the man suddenly felt the stick fly from his hand. Then, before he could regain his self-possession, two boyish figures crouched swiftly one on each side of him.

Dexter felt his knees gripped. In the same instant two boys rose suddenly, holding on, and the bully toppled over backward.

"Never hit a man when he's down," quoth the dry voice of Greg Holmes. "But, if he isn't even any sort of a man, it doesn't matter!"

Thump! Greg brought his not very big fist down on Dexter's nose. It was an ugly blow, delivered before the bully could recover from his own amazement.

Dave Darrin, the other boy, did not even wait to speak. He began to rain down blows on the prostrate enemy.

"Here, stop that, Davey!" urged Dick, darting forward. "Don't hit the cur any more."

"But he was going to club you," argued Dave, hitting two more blows.

"Stop this, boys! Let up! I'll clear out," begged Ab. Dexter.

Dick, finding that neither of his chums was much inclined to stop the merited punishment, darted in and forcibly dragged Darrin off Dexter's prostrate form.

"Let me have him, for a minute or two yet," coaxed Greg Holmes. "You know, Dick, he was going to club you."

"I know it," rejoined young Prescott doggedly. "He did thrash me twice, and it hurt. I don't believe in soiling our hands on anything like this fellow, when it can be helped. Besides, we're too many."

Though Dave and Greg had now both been pulled off their prey, they hovered over Dexter, who seemed afraid to rise for fear it would lead to a renewed onslaught.

"Stand back, fellows," coaxed Dick, pushing them gently. "Dexter, I told you you'd be a booby in any fight where you couldn't have it all your own way. I was right about it. Get up, now—and make your fly-away while I'm still able to hold these two bulldogs in leash. Hustle now!"

Dick emphasized his advice with a kick, but it was not a vicious one. Ab. Dexter looked up in wonder. Then he rose, crouchingly, next made a sprinter's start and bolted.

"Humph! We can never get him now," uttered Dave Darrin disgustedly. "Whew! I wish I could run as fast as that."

"You can learn," replied Dick.

"Yes; in about ten years!"

"Dave, you could learn to run a heap faster than you do, and in a mighty short time."

"How?"

"Just start in to train. Get someone who knows something about it to give you pointers on running. Pshaw! I believe our whole crowd ought to start in to learn to run. To run, really, I mean. If I had been a faster runner to-night I might have gotten away from that bully. I might have saved myself from a good many aches that I've got just now."

"You aching?" questioned Darrin. "What makes you ache?"

"Dexter gave me two hard thrashings before you fellows got along."

"He did?" sputtered Dave vengefully. "O Dick, why did you ever let him get away from us?"

"I'm glad I did something to the sneak while I had the chance," declared Greg Holmes.

"First of all, tell me how you fellows came to find me," suggested Dick Prescott.

"Oh, that's easy enough to account for," Dave replied. "Greg and I were on Main Street looking for you. Then we went down to the store. Your mother told us that you'd gone to Mrs. Davis's with a package of books, so we set out to meet you on your return. And right over there, on the street, we came across a little girl, white, scared and half crying. She said she had seen a man grab you up, throw you over the wall——"

"Yes, that happened," nodded Prescott.

"And the little kiddie said she saw the man jump over the wall, grab you up and start for the woods. She was sure the wicked man was going to kill you."

"Dexter was mad enough, but he lacked the sand for going that far, I guess," remarked Prescott.

"He might not be without the sand," argued Dave. "I've got a notion that Dexter, while a coward, perhaps, about some things, would go about as far as his anger drove him. I'm glad we came along, anyway."

"So am I. You fellows sneaked in so quietly in the dark, that I didn't see you until just before you tackled Dexter. Well, there's no great harm done, thanks to you, Dave, and to you, Greg. Let's get back to Main Street."

As the youngsters crossed the field and strolled up the street, Dick gave an accurate account of what had befallen him.

"So the sneak wanted to pay you to help him in some dirty sort of work?" demanded Dave, his dark eyes ablaze with disgust.

"I imagine it must have been dirty work, since Dexter had planned it out," Dick admitted, smiling.

"The hound! But then, see here, Dick; if Dexter wanted you to help him in anything of that sort, it means that he's going to try to bother that poor wife of his again."

"It looks that way, Dave."

"Then we ought to warn Mrs. Dexter, so that she can be on her guard against the worthless rascal."

"I've been thinking of that, Dave. Yes; I'm sure we must go and give Mrs. Dexter a hint. It wouldn't be right not to tell her of what may be ahead of her."

"We might go around to her house to-morrow afternoon after school, eh?" proposed Greg.

"Football practice to-morrow afternoon," retorted Dave Darrin dryly.

"Besides, to-morrow afternoon might be too late," urged Dick. "Fellows, when we have a message like this, which may be of great importance to some other human being, there's no time for doing the errand like—*now*!"

"That's right, too," approved Dave. "It won't take us more than five minutes to reach Mrs. Dexter's house. Let's head for there at the next corner?"

That being agreed to, the three chums set out at a brisk walk. A few minutes later Dick was pulling the doorbell of Mrs. Dexter's new home, while Dave and Greg stood just a little below him on the steps.

It was a pretty little house, of ten rooms; not as large a house as Mrs. Dexter might have been able to afford, but one that was a happy contrast to the three-room flat in which Mrs. Dexter had lived when obliged to support herself at dressmaking. As yet there were but two servants on the place—a woman who did the house-work and a hired man, who slept in a room over the little barn at the rear of the house.

"Will you ask Mrs. Dexter if she can see us, please?" asked Dick, lifting his cap, when the woman-of-all-work opened the door. "Kindly tell her that we have news for her which we think may be very important."

"Come in, boys," replied the housekeeper, doubtless pleased by Dick's deference in raising his cap, an example in which he had been promptly followed by Dave and Greg.

The woman showed them into a little parlor. Mrs. Dexter soon came down and greeted them.

"I'm very glad you boys have called on me," she said. "You and your other friends did me a service to-day that I can't forget. I was on the way to the bank to leave the jewels and the money when you helped me so handsomely."

"We've come, Mrs. Dexter," said Dick, "to tell you what happened to-night. It may be the means of saving you from further trouble with Mr. Dexter."

Then Dick told the story of his adventure that evening. Dave and Greg added a few words at the end.

"So we think," summed up Dick, "that Mr. Dexter may not yet be through with his schemes against you. Excuse us, Mrs. Dexter, but don't you think it would be well to have a man sleep in the house—one that you can depend on if Dexter comes here to make trouble?"

"Yes, indeed. My hired man is a straight-forward fellow. I'll have him stay around here more, and I'll have a room fitted up in the house for him. Mr. Dexter isn't usually extremely brave. I imagine that the hired man can take care of him if he puts in an appearance. At all events, I shall feel safer for having a man in the house."

Their errand being done, the three Grammar School boys would have risen to go, but Mrs. Dexter detained them, asking many questions about their school life.

Then, somehow, the story came out of the newly organized Central Grammar football squad.

"Oh, but that is going to be fine!" cried Mrs. Dexter. "Manly sports always make boys stronger, and give them a better sense of fair play when such a sense is needed. You'll have uniforms, of course. What will your uniforms be like?"

"That's one of the points we haven't decided on yet," smiled Dick. "The uniforms will have to come, in good time."

"Your football organization has a treasurer, of course?"

"He's a luxury we don't need yet," laughed Dave.

"Why not?"

"Because there isn't any treasury."

"Yet there will be, of course—that is, if——"

Suddenly Mrs. Dexter looked mightily pleased and clapped her hands.

"I've stumbled on to one of your secrets, boys," she cried. "You haven't any treasury, and you're still wondering where the money can come from to pay for uniforms. Well, you needn't wonder any longer. All of you boys who helped me to-day are interested in the football plan. You did me a very great service to-day, and you've done me another one to-night. Now I'm going to buy the football uniforms. How much will they cost—ten dollars apiece?"

"Five or six ought to buy as good uniforms as we'll need," replied Dick Prescott, reddening. "But, Mrs. Dexter, we don't want——"

"Let me have my own way, won't you?" she pleaded plaintively. "It's such a very new thing for me to be able to have my own way. I'm going to write the check, to-night, to pay for the uniforms. Don't stop me, please don't."

Mrs. Dexter rose and went over to a little desk, where she sat fingering her checkbook.

"Now please give me some idea of what such uniforms cost. I want to do it nicely for you boys. Excuse me just a moment, though."

Mrs. Dexter touched a bell on her desk and the housekeeper entered.

"Jane, when I put Myra to bed this evening, she showed signs of a cough. I don't want the child to get croupy and not know anything about it. Just run up and watch Myra, won't you, without waking her? Then come down and let me know, after a few minutes."

The housekeeper started upstairs. Mrs. Dexter returned to the subject of football uniforms, while the three boys, red-faced and reluctant, answered her questions. They appreciated her kindness, but they did not want her to pay for the uniforms. To Dick and his chums it looked too much like begging.

A shriek sounded upstairs. Then Jane came rushing down.

"Oh, ma'am!" she cried in dismay. "Myra's gone—her bed's empty, and the clothes that she wore have been taken from the chair!"

While Mrs. Dexter turned deathly pale and tottered, Dick Prescott leaped up, exclaiming:

"It's the work of Dexter. That's the scheme he had!"

CHAPTER VI

ON THE TRAIL OF THE CAB

"The wretch has stolen Myra! I didn't I think he would dare do that,"cried the woman.

Mrs. Dexter had never made any effort to secure a divorce from her worthless husband. After he had abandoned her she had appeared in court and had had herself appointed sole guardian and custodian of little Myra. Under the law, therefore, Dexter, if he stole Myra away from the mother, could be arrested and punished for abduction.

At this frantic moment, however, Mrs. Dexter was not thinking of punishments. All she wanted was to get her child back in her own keeping.

"Isn't it possible there's a mistake?" demanded Greg of the dismayed housekeeper. "The little one may have gotten up out of bed. She may be in some other part of the house."

"Not much!" interjected the housekeeper. "The child's jacket and coat are gone from a hook near by."

After the first moment of fright Mrs. Dexter had raced upstairs; now she came down again.

"Myra's really gone," she cried, sobbing. "And no one but Dexter would think of stealing her from me. He has done it for spite—or as the means of extorting more money from me."

"A man could hardly go through the streets carrying a child that didn't want to be carried. The child could cry out and attract attention," guessed Dick.

"Myra wouldn't cry out. She would be cowed by her father's threats. She always was afraid of him," wailed Mrs. Dexter.

"Are you going to appeal to the police?" Dick asked.

"I—I must."

"Then you're losing time, Mrs. Dexter—and there's your telephone. We boys will go out into the streets and see if we can find any trace—pick up any word. When we came along there was a cab standing in front of the Grahams. But I suppose that cab belonged to some of their visitors."

"The Grahams have been out of town for the last few days," broke in Mrs.

Dexter. "There has been no one at their house, except one old man who acts as care-taker."

"Then Dexter may have had that cab waiting for him," flashed young Prescott. "Come along, fellows! Let's see what we can find out."

Dave and Greg were at the street door ahead of their young leader. None of the boys paused longer, for Mrs. Dexter was already at hertelephone.

Out in the street the three Grammar School lads raced along the sidewalk until they reached the house of the Graham family. The cab was gone.

"We can find that cab anywhere," declared Dick. "Any one else would recognize it. It had one brown, or dark horse, and one gray horse."

"I didn't notice the driver," stated Darrin.

"He was sitting inside the cab," spoke up Greg. "I didn't get a good look at him, either."

"Going to race on into Main Street?" asked Dave, as the three came to a street corner.

"Dexter would hardly drive right into the clutches of the police, would he?" pondered Prescott. "No; I think it'll turn out that he went the opposite way, out of town."

Saying this, Dick headed for the outskirts of Gridley, still keeping along at a dog-trot. Dave and Greg didn't talk now; they were husbanding their store of "wind."

After a short time all three boys had to slow down to a walk. That "pain in the side," which seizes all boys who try to run far without training and practice, had caught them. Still, they moved along as fast as they could go.

"Excuse me, mister," hailed Dick, halting the first man they met, who came strolling toward them, smoking a pipe, "have you seen a cab go by?"

"Yes."

"Oldish cab?" broke in Dave.

"One gray horse and one dark or brown?" breathed Greg.

"Yep."

"How long ago?" asked all three.

"'Bout two minutes ago. Why?"

"Which way did it go?" breathed Dick anxiously.

"Why, the driver stopped me," explained the man, taking out his pipe, "and asked if there was a drug store ahead in this part of the town. I told him he'd find one on the next block, around the next corner to the left. So——"

"Thank you!" came politely from three breathless boys, and off they started again on a trot.

"Any one sick?" called the man after them. "Huh! Curious how excited those boys are!"

"Two minutes! I'm afraid horses will leave us far behind with that start," groaned Dick.

Then they turned around the corner. Ahead of them, in front of the little drug store, or rather, just past the entrance, stood the cab that occupied all their thoughts at the present time.

"There it is!" breathed Dick excitedly, as though forgetful of the fact that his chums had eyes also. "Come along—over on the other side of the street—in the dark."

In a twinkling all three lads had crossed stealthily to the further side of the little street.

"Oh, for a policeman!" appealed Dick. "Or any full-grown man, who would listen to us and have the grit to give us a strong hand."

"If Dexter has the little girl, and that's his cab, what has he taken her into a drug store for?" whispered Dave.

"We don't know that he has taken her into the store. We don't know anything until we see it," was Dick's answer. "Dexter didn't stop for a trifle. He isn't buying Myra a glass of soda, or anything like that."

The three boys were stealing down the street, on the further side, keeping close in the shadow of the buildings. They did not wish to risk being seen until they had had a chance for a good look at the cab and its possible contents.

Dick's reason for crossing the street had been that he had first caught sight of the driver standing on the sidewalk beside the cab. If he could get down close to the cab, and have that vehicle between himself and the driver, Dick hoped that he would have a chance to steal across the street and look inside the rig.

By good luck, combined with stealth, Dick, Dave and Greg succeeded in gaining a point on the street opposite the cab.

"Careful, now," whispered Dick, "one bad move might spoil everything."

On tip-toe they crossed. At a point midway in the street they halted a brief instant. From this point they could make out the unmistakable form of Ab. Dexter at the back of the drug store, walking to and fro as if waiting for something.

No word was spoken. Still on tip-toe the boys went on until they stood by one of the doors of the cab.

Dave and Greg made way for Dick to get up close and peer into the vehicle.

Young Prescott gave a start of exultation as he made out a little, wrapped-up human bundle huddled on the back seat. It was little four-year-old Myra. She had collapsed into a heap and was very softly sobbing to herself, wholly unaware of what might be passing outside.

On the further side of the cab, standing on the sidewalk, Dick caught sight of the man whom he presumed to be the driver. The fellow was standing staring fixedly ahead.

"If he had been looking the other way he would have caught us coming down the street," flashed through Prescott's mind.

Then he turned, nodding swiftly, silently, at his companions.

They had found Myra, these Grammar School lads, but in a desperate fight, Dexter and the driver would prove overwhelming odds. The pair of rascals could knock these youngsters senseless and whip up the horses for a dash.

What was to be done?

In sheer nervousness Dave Darrin began to try the handle of the cab door. Then, understanding coming to him, Dave tried in earnest to see whether he could unfasten the door with out making the least noise.

All three of the lads realized that it was a ticklish moment. Even Myra, if startled, might give the scream that would betray and defeat them.

Steadily Dave worked at his problem. Dick and Greg, quivering, stood alertly on guard on either side of him.

Squeak! That cab-door handle needed oiling sadly. Even under Darrin's cautious handling it gave forth a noise that sounded startling in the stillness.

"What's that?" they heard the driver mutter, as he started. Then came the sound of footsteps, as the driver wheeled and ran around behind the cab.

He was bearing down straight upon them!

CHAPTER VII

DICK LEADS A SPIRITED RUSH

"Hustle, Dave—into the cab!" shouted Dick Prescott lustily.

Darrin obeyed like a flash, pulling the door shut.

"What are you young monkeys doing here?" yelled the driver hoarsely. Then, as he caught better sight of them, he snarled:

"Oh, I know you boys! You belong to the Butt-insky family!"

The driver's next remark was "ouch!" as Greg darted in and struck him fairly at the belt line. In the same instant young Prescott managed to trip the fellow.

"Boss!" bawled the driver, as he struck the pavement.

"Into the cab with you, Greg!" shouted Dick.

Dave swung the door open, and in the same instant Greg bolted inside, while Dick Prescott made a single bound at the front wheel, from which he mounted to the driver's seat.

"None of that!" yelled the driver, getting upon his feet and moving forward. At the same moment another man came to the door of the drug store.

That man was—must have been—Abner Dexter. He wore the same clothes that Dick remembered, but over his head and face were drawn a wig and beard that made him look some one else.

Whish! Dick's left hand clutched at the reins, but his right hand grasped the whip. That useful implement described an arc downward and caught the driver roundly, judging by the yell that the fellow let out.

The Whip Caught the Driver Roundly.

"Gid-dap!" yelled young Prescott, completing the swing of the whip by bringing it down across the horses' backs.

The startled animals leaped forward, the lurch almost throwing Dick from the box; in fact, it nearly overturned the cab.

But the vehicle soon righted itself, and Dick, somewhat scared, yet steady, pulled the horses down to a steady trot and reined them in closer together.

The disguised man who had come out of the drug store succeeded in resting one hand for an instant on the body of the cab. But the springing horses carried it away from him. For a few rods the man pursued, the smarting driver bringing up the rear.

Then both pursuers halted, panting, cursing, at the same time, as only foul-mouthed ruffians can.

Inside, Myra was shrieking with fright.

"We're your mother's friends, Myra, and are taking you back to her," explained Dave, holding the small child on his knee and trying to quiet her.

Greg Holmes, in the meantime, was more concerned with looking out of the window.

"Why, say," muttered Greg. "Dick ain't driving to Mrs. Dexter's, not by a long shot. He seems to be heading straight into the business part of the town."

"You leave Dick Prescott alone to know what he's doing," advised Dave

Darrin calmly.

"Yes; I guess that's right," assented Greg.

"Dick is the longest-headed fellow in our school."

"Except me," grinned Greg modestly.

"You? Huh! I'm glad you're not outside on the box."

"I reckon it's the first time Dick ever drove cab horses."

"He'll do it right, anyway."

"But I wonder why he isn't going to the Dexter house," pursued young Holmes.

Then Myra took fright again.

"Take me home!" she cried. "I want to see my mamma!"

From that she passed into wild sobbing, taxing all Dave Darrin's powers to ease her mind.

"You're going home, Myra," he wound up. "You're going to see your mother."

"My papa is a bad man!"

"Well, he's not here now," smiled Dave. "Did you ever hear of Dick Prescott?"

"Yes; he's a nice boy."

"You're right he is," added Dave with enthusiasm. "Well, Dick is up outside, driving the horses, and he'll take us home by the way that it's best to go."

"Here we are in Main Street," announced Greg wonderingly.

Dave thought he began to understand Prescott's plan, but he said nothing. A few moments later the cab turned down one of the side streets, then halted before a cluster of lights.

"The police station!" exploded Greg.

"Of course," nodded Dave.

"Why 'of course'?"

"Because it's part of Dick's plan."

"Come out, fellows," called Dick. "We're at the end of our trip, thank goodness."

Greg opened the door, Dave stepping out with Myra in his arms.

"My mamma doesn't live here," cried the child uneasily.

"No, but it's all right," Dave urged soothingly. "You come right along and see if it isn't."

Dick led the way up the police-station steps. In the office three uniformed members of the force were talking excitedly. One of them was the night lieutenant, Janeway.

"I tell you, Lieutenant, the thing was done so slickly that the child ain't going to be found to-night," one of the patrolmen was saying.

"If you're talking about Myra Dexter, guess again," laughed young Prescott. "Here she is now."

Three astounded policemen turned to regard the happy-faced Grammar School boys.

"Then she wasn't stolen at all?" demanded one of the patrolmen. "Just strolled away and got lost, eh?"

"Oh, no!" Dick retorted. "Myra was stolen, all right; but we stole her back again."

"How?"

"We took her away from her father and a cab-driver," chuckled Greg Holmes.

"Stop telling us any nonsense like that," interposed the lieutenant sternly. "Tell us where you found the child."

Dick related the story briefly. The policemen were at first inclined to doubt the story, but one of them glanced outside and saw the cab.

"If you'll let me offer a suggestion," went on Dick, "there's a mother at home who is nearly crazy with grief. Hadn't you better call Mrs. Dexter on the telephone and tell her that Myra is safe with you?"

The lieutenant quickly wheeled to his 'phone, calling for Mrs. Dexter's number. One of the policemen, in the meantime, received Myra in his arms.

"Mrs. Dexter?" called the lieutenant into the transmitter. "This is the police station. We have your little girl here, all safe and sound. How was she found? Three schoolboys, Dick Prescott, Dave Dar—— Oh, you know the names? Well, they trailed the cab to where it had stopped outside of a drug store. They knocked the driver down and got away with the cab. How did three boys manage to do such a deed? Wait! I'll let Master Prescott himself tell you over the 'phone."

The lieutenant wheeled about.

"Where in the name of mischief are those boys?" he demanded. The two policemen turned in equal confusion. Certain it was that the Grammar School boys had bolted.

So the lieutenant sent out to find a driver, and one of his policemen got inside with Myra, to take her home. The policeman was also instructed to remain on guard outside through the night, in case Dexter and his confederate should feel inclined to make another attempt to abduct the little one.

Dick and his chums, after leaving the station house silently, had run until they found themselves around the corner on Main Street.

"We don't want to be thanked any more by Mrs. Dexter to-night," Dick ventured to his friends.

"We certainly don't," agreed Dave.

"What'll we do now?" asked Greg.

"We'll go home," suggested young Prescott. "Our folks will be wondering where we are."

"Whee! But we'll have a lot to tell the folks!" chuckled Greg. "When my mother hears what we've been through to-night the chances are ten to one that she'll make me stay in nights."

"Not if she pauses to think what you did to help another mother out," hinted Dave.

"Well, good night, fellows," called Dick as he reached his corner. "We've had a bully time, but that won't get us up early in the morning."

The bookstore was due to close at nine o'clock, but it was twenty-five minutes after that hour when Dick swung in through the front door.

"Mother, here's the boy," called Mr. Prescott, being the first to espy the returning son. "Young man, you'll have to give your mother a good account of yourself. She's been worrying about you."

"Oh, I knew Dick was in no great danger," laughed Mrs. Prescott, coming forward to kiss her son, now that her worry had ended pleasantly. "But, Richard, you're still a bit young to stay out so late."

"I suppose, mother, that depends a bit upon what I've been doing, doesn't it?"

"Why, has anything happened out of the usual?"

"I'll tell you about it," agreed the lad.

"Wait until I put up the shutters and lock the door," directed his father. "Then we'll all go upstairs."

Gathered on the floor above, the Prescotts listened in amazement to what their son narrated.

"Why, I never heard of so much happening before in one day," gasped Mrs. Prescott.

"It never happened to me, before, anyway," laughed Dick. "However, I hope I've brought home a good excuse for being out a little late."

"Dick," broke in his father solemnly, "the next time any such train of events happens you have my permission to be out until—let me see. Well, say, until quarter of ten. But don't let such things happen too often. And now, to bed with you!"

"Dick is not going to bed just yet," interposed his mother. "A boy who has been as active as he has to-night is bound to be hungry. Come with me to the pantry."

CHAPTER VIII

TWO ACCIDENTS—OR TRAPS?

Before Gridley left its breakfast tables the following morning Dick Prescott and his chums were rather famous.

For the editor of the "Blade" had played up the Dexter abduction for the big local story in the morning's issue.

Dick saw it, of course, and felt a curious thrill when he saw his own name in big block type. The names of Dave and Greg were also there.

"I'll read the yarn to you while you eat," smiled his father. "This is a great day for you, lad. You're tasting, for the first time, the sensation of looming large in the public eye."

Dick read the story over twice for himself before starting for school. Yet the first thrill was missing.

"Pshaw! Len Spencer, or someone, has made a hero tale out of a boys' lark," muttered the Grammar School boy. "It sounded fine, at first, but that just shows how ready a fellow is to believe he's smarter than other folks. Whee! But we'll get a choice lot of teasing out of the fellows at school to-day!"

Prescott was glad, that morning, that he contrived to pick up Dave and Greg on the way to school.

"Get yourselves braced," Dick warned his friends. "All the fellows will be out to roast us for being 'heroes.' Oh, we'll catch it."

No sooner had the three turned the corner that led down to the school than one of their class-mates "spotted" them.

"Here come Dick & Co!" roared the discoverer. "Turn out! Give 'em a welcome! Dick & Co.—lost children trapped and trained! See the real, bony-fido heroes! 'Ray! Now, then, altogether—*ouch!*"

The spouter found himself suddenly flat on his back on the sidewalk, having been sent there by a vigorous trip from Tom Reade.

"All that ails you, Hen Dutcher, is that you didn't get your name in the paper," called Tom denouncingly. "But you will, one of these days. It'll be in the police-court news, though. Sixty days for vagrancy!"

"Say, do you know what I'll do to you?" demanded young Dutcher, clenching his fists and advancing upon Reade.

"Nothing," asserted Tom calmly. "That's all you ever do, except make a noise with your mouth. I never hear your mouth making any noise, though, when recitation in arithmetic is going on."

"You think you're smart, don't you?" glowered Hen Dutcher.

"I don't think you are, anyway," retorted Tom, turning on his heel.

Dan Dalzell and Harry Hazelton were at hand, and now the whole of Dick & Co. presented a rather solid front. Some of the other boys wanted to do some "guying," but Tom's prompt and vigorous rebuke to Dutcher had cooled the ardor of a lot of would-be teasers.

The bell rang soon, calling all inside. School opened as usual, but after a little Old Dut glanced up, looking keenly at Dick and two of the latter's friends.

"I am glad to be able to tell you all," began the principal, "that three of my boys, last night——"

As he paused all eyes were turned toward three boys who were turning different shades of red.

"Three of my boys," continued Old Dut, "did their school credit by displaying the qualities of good citizenship. You all know whom I mean. Master Prescott, do you care to rise and tell us something of the events of last night?"

"I'd rather not, sir," pleaded Prescott.

"Master Darrin?" pursued Old Dut.

"I feel like Master Prescott, only more so," replied Dave, turning redder still.

"Master Holmes?"

"By the advice of my lawyer," rejoined Greg solemnly, "I have nothing to say."

"I'm glad to see that our young men are modest, as well as brave," continued Old Dut.

Some of the boys had been staring expectantly, some of the girls admiringly. Laura Bentley, the doctor's daughter, looked secretly pleased when she heard Dick decline to tell of his adventures.

"First class in American history will now recite," announced Old Dut, and the work of the day had begun. Yet, somehow, most of the pupils seemed to have forgotten whatever they had previously known of the campaign against Richmond.

At recess Dick, Dave and Greg, flanked by their three other chums, managed to keep clear of tormentors.

When school was out at noon, however, one boy called out:

"Are we going to have football practice this afternoon, Dick?"

"He can't waste the time," sang out Hen Dutcher derisively. "He has a job going a-heroing."

Tom Reade turned sharply, but this time there was no need of his darting at the tormentor. Six boys had promptly caught up Hen—two by the legs, two at the body and two more at the shoulders. Rushing Hen to the nearest tree, they promptly and soundly spanked him by the very simple method of holding his legs apart and swinging his body smartly against the tree-trunk.

"You kids think ye're smart!" growled Hen ruefully, as he rubbed himself.

"Everyone knows you're not, Hen," retorted one of the late spankers. "You're only stupidly fresh."

Hen quickly subsided and vanished.

"Yes; we ought to have football practice this afternoon," Dick answered, when the question was put to him again. "We have no time to lose if we're going to play this season. How many of you fellows have studied the rules?"

"I have," answered several.

"But, say," broke in one boy, "we can just as well give up the idea of having uniforms. We fellows can't raise the cash."

"Mrs. Dexter has offered to buy the uniforms," put in Greg incautiously.

"Has she?"

A whoop of delight went up from some of the boys.

"She'll be able to buy us bully ones; she has lots of money these days," declared one listener.

"Yes; Mrs. Dexter offered to supply the money," Dick admitted. "But, fellows, I want you all to think that over. I, for one, shall vote against getting our uniforms that way."

"Why?" came a chorus.

"Because, fellows, if we haven't brains and industry enough to get our uniforms ourselves we've no business togging up at all. We can play pretty good football, for that matter, with nothing but the ball itself."

Some sided with Dick; others were in favor of letting any one who was willing provide the field togs for the Central Grammar School eleven.

Dick didn't stop to argue long. He was hungry for his dinner. On Main Street he parted from his chums, pursuing his way home alone. He had not gone far when he had to pass a new building in process of erection. Three stories had already been built up, and the workmen were now engaged in putting on the fourth and last story.

Dick was just passing the main entrance of the new building when he heard a warning rattle above. Instinct made him dart into the entrance.

Nor did he move an instant too soon. Some thirty bricks fell to the sidewalk with a great clatter. Among them landed a heavy hod.

"My! But that was a close shave!" quivered the boy. "A second or two later and my head would have been split open!"

He darted out, but did not stop until he had reached the middle of the road.

"Hey!" Prescott shouted up to the top of the building, but no one answered.

"Be careful, up there, where you dump your bricks!" called Dick once more.

A customer coming out of a store next door caught sight of the bricks and the hod.

"What's the matter, Prescott?" called the man.

"Some workman was careless, and let that hod and all the bricks fall," Dick answered. "I heard them coming, and got in out of the shower just in time."

"No workman did that," muttered the man, after staring in bewilderment for a moment. "The men are all off, getting their dinner."

"Then who could have done it?" Dick wanted to know.

"Humph! If you have any enemies, Prescott, I'd say that trick was done by some one who didn't care how badly you were hurt."

"Oh, nonsense!" rejoined Dick. "I don't believe any one hates me badly enough to do a thing like that."

"Didn't you have some trouble with a couple of men yesterday?"

"Why, yes; but——"

Dick halted suddenly, looking puzzled. Could it be possible, after all, that this was a "delicate" attention from Ab. Dexter?

For Dexter had no need to be afraid of walking the streets of Gridley. His wife had refused to procure a warrant for him on the charge of attempted abduction of Myra. She was unwilling that her child should bear the disgrace of having a father in prison.

Three other men had drawn close and halted. To them the first man explained what had happened.

"Come on!" cried one of the newcomers, hastening into the building. "One of you stay out on the sidewalk; another go to the back of the building. We'll soon find out whether there's any one in the building."

Dick joined, as the person most interested, in the swift, thorough search that was made.

No other human being than the searchers, however, was to be found in the building.

"I don't believe any one threw it at me," said Dick thoughtfully, after all hands had returned to the street. "The hod must have been left standing near the edge of the building—perhaps against the top of a ladder. Then the breeze up there may have jarred it out of place. At any rate, I'm not hurt, and no harm is done. But I wish to thank all of you gentlemen for taking the trouble to make the search."

"Humph!" muttered one of the men, after Dick had hurried away. "The idea of a hod being left standing, and then being blown over into the street doesn't satisfy me!"

Dick was late reaching home. What he had in the way of dinner he had to force down hurriedly, and then start for school once more.

After school that afternoon most of the boys of seventh and eighth grades turned up at the field, eager for more football work.

"It seems to me," announced Dick thoughtfully, "that there is no sense in kicking a ball around the field aimlessly. There isn't much use in rushes or mass plays, either, until we know what we are doing and can do it according to the rules. So, fellows, what do you say to seeing who knows the rules best? Let's have a drill in rules."

Many of the youngsters objected to that as being too tame. Yet Dick's idea carried the day, after all. Some of the fellows went away, thinking this sort of procedure too much like a lesson and too little like fun. After nearly an hour's discussion of the rules two elevens were formed and there was time for some play.

Dick & Co. left the field together. On the way home young Prescott spoke of the falling of the bricks at noon.

"That wasn't any accident," spoke up Dave, with an air of great conviction.

"You think some one did that on purpose?"

"I'm sure of it," Dave asserted.

"Who could have done it?"

"Who but Ab. Dexter?"

"Wrong!" volunteered Tom Reade. "Up at the field a man in a buggy hauled up to watch the play. He happened to mention that he had seen Dexter over in Stayton this noon. Stayton is nine miles away from here."

"Then of course it wasn't Dexter," declared Dick.

"It must have been that other fellow," suggested Greg.

"You mean that special officer, Driggs?" inquired Dick.

"Of course. And I'll tell you where else we saw that fellow Driggs. He was the driver of the cab last night. I've just placed that voice ofhis."

"Then Driggs was disguised last night, the same as Dexter was."

"Of course."

"And I can tell you something else," continued Tom Reade. "I know what Dexter was doing in the drug store last night. I met Len Spencer this noon. Len had been investigating."

"What did Dexter want in the drug store?" asked Prescott.

"Soothing syrup. Len says he guesses that Ab. Dexter was afraid Myra would make too much noise before he got through the night, and that Dexter must have meant to drug the child into quietness."

"It ought not to have taken Dexter all that time just to get a bottle of soothing syrup," suggested Prescott.

"It did, in this case," Reade declared. "The druggist thought there was something queer in Dexter's manner, and so he questioned him sharply as to what Dexter wanted to do with the stuff. Dexter got confused, next angry, and the druggist had about made up his mind not to sell the stuff."

"Well, I hope we've heard the last of that precious pair, Driggs and

Dexter," murmured Dalzell plaintively.

"Mrs. Dexter holds the key to that situation," remarked Dick thoughtfully. "If she lets Dexter have money, from time to time, he'll still hang around. If she won't let him have money, and has herself guarded from him, then by and by he'll get tired. Then he'll clear out for new scenes and try some other scheme of getting a living without working. Mrs. Dexter——"

"Sh!" warned Harry Hazelton. "Speaking of angels, here she comes now."

"Boys, I've been looking for you," cried Mrs. Dexter, halting before them. "We didn't come to an understanding last night about the uniforms for your football team."

"How's Myra to-day?" asked Dick, anxious to shelve the other topic.

"She's all right to-day, except that the child is very nervous. That is natural, of course, after her bad scare last night."

"Aren't you afraid to leave her alone?"

"Myra isn't alone. She has Jane to look after her, and Special Officer Grimsby is in the house. I have hired Mr. Grimsby to live at my house for the present. He's a brave man, and will stop any nonsense that may be tried by certain people."

"Well, we must be getting along," urged Prescott. "It is very near our supper time, and——"

"But about the uniforms?" persisted Mrs. Dexter.

"Mrs. Dexter, the fellows appreciate your offer very highly. It pleased them all to know that you made it."

"I'm glad to hear that," smiled Mrs. Dexter.

"But, ma'am," Prescott continued just as earnestly, "while the fellows all feel extremely grateful, they would rather you didn't think of doing anything of the sort. The fellows feel that if they're smart enough to wear football uniforms, they're smart enough to get 'em. It would take all feeling of hustle out of the team if some one else smoothed the way for them like that."

"I see," half assented Mrs. Dexter reluctantly.

"Therefore, ma'am, if you will accept our gratitude for your offer, and agree to the notion of the fellows that they'll do best if they do their own hustling, we'll all be mightily pleased as well as grateful."

"Oh, well, then," replied the good woman, "we'll simply consider that the matter is postponed. I can't agree, as easily as this, to drop what I have considered my privilege."

As soon as could be, Dick & Co. made their escape.

They met again for a little while in the evening. Nothing of any real moment happened while they were together.

While Dave Darrin was on his way home, however, and going along a dark part of the street, something whizzed by his head, striking the sidewalk just ahead.

"Quit your fooling!" yelled Dave, wheeling about angrily.

No human being, however, was in sight. Dave ran back, some two hundred feet in all, but could see no one on the little street, nor in any hiding place near by.

Then Dave went back to inspect the missile. It was a stone, slightly larger than his two fists together.

"Whew!" whistled Dave inwardly. "That thing wasn't meant for any joke, either!"

CHAPTER IX

AN AWESOME RIVER DISCOVERY

"Want to come, fellows?" asked Greg, halting Dick and Dave on Main Street Saturday morning.

"Where?" asked Dick.

"Jim Haynes told me I might take his big canoe this morning."

"So you're going canoeing?" queried Dave.

"Yep; and better'n that, too," glowed Greg. "You know Payson, the farmer, up the river?"

"Of course."

"This being an apple year, Payson told me I could have a few barrels of apples if I'd pick 'em and pay him twenty cents a barrel. His orchard is right along the river bank. Isn't that a cinch?"

"I'd like to go," rejoined Dick wistfully. "But I can't, very well. You see, I've got to work in the store this afternoon. Dad is going to be away."

"Your mother'll let you go, if you tell her what a fine time you can have."

"That wouldn't be quite fair," replied Dick, shaking his head. "Mother would let me go, I know; but the trouble with her," he added, with a smile, "is that she's always too easy. And I know there's more work to do in the store this afternoon than she can handle alone."

"I'd go in a minute," Dave chipped in, "but you see I've agreed to go to the express office this afternoon and help check up bundles. I'm to get a quarter for it."

"Huh," returned Greg candidly. "I'm disappointed about you two. It takes money to buy apples, even at twenty cents a barrel. You two generally have some money."

"I've got five cents," laughed Dave. "Here it is."

"I've got a whole quarter, as it happens," added Dick, producing the coin. "I'm not going to be mean, either."

"Whew, but I'll have a job pulling the canoe alone," muttered Greg ruefully. "And it isn't much fun picking apples all alone. However, I'm going. Maybe Harry Hazelton can go with me. Tom can't and Dan won't. I'll see that you two get your shares of apples for the money you've turned over to me."

"My share will be half a hat full," laughed Dave.

"And then some more, and still some more," added Greg readily. "I won't forget that you two financed my expedition."

"I wish awfully that I could go with you, Greg," spoke Dick truthfully. "But it wouldn't be fair for me to think of leaving everything at the store for mother to do this afternoon."

"Oh, that's all right," nodded Greg.

"And you can bet that I wish I were going with you," supplemented Darrin. "But I get a lot of snaps like this one at the express office, and there are too many fellows hanging around there looking for my chance. It isn't the easiest thing in the world for a fellow to pick up silver quarters, Greg."

"Don't I know!" muttered Holmes.

So Greg went on his way.

"Say, wouldn't that be a great way to put in the afternoon?" sighed Dave. "These fine September days get into a fellow's blood and make him itch for the river and the fields."

"Don't tempt me," begged Dick Prescott plaintively. "I'm trying to do the square thing by mother, and I do want to go with Greg!"

"Oh, well, a fellow can't always act on the square and have a good time, too," philosophized Dave. "On the whole, I guess I'd rather have the satisfaction of acting on the square."

Afternoon toil brought its rewards, however. Five members of Dick & Co., released from further responsibilities, met as usual on Main Street that evening. They strolled about, met other fellows from the Central Grammar, discussed football and talked over all the other topics dear to the hearts of Grammar School boys.

"I wonder how Greg got along this afternoon?" suggested Dave. "Any of you hear?"

The others shook their heads.

"We could go down to his house and ask him, only it would look as though we were just hunting for apples," said Dick.

"Oh, Greg knows us better'n that," declared Tom Reade. "And Greg will simply bring the apples to us, if we don't go to his house. What' say if we take a trip down Greg's way? Maybe we'll meet him coming up to find the crowd."

This counsel prevailing, the five set out on a direct walk to Greg's home. A block away they met Mr. Holmes coming in their direction.

"You're just the ones I wanted to see, boys," was Mr. Holmes's greeting. "Where's Greg?"

"We were going down to the house to find him, sir," Dick responded.

"I'm a good deal worried," confessed Mr. Holmes. "Greg went up river this afternoon, after apples, and he hasn't been home yet."

"Not home yet?" gasped Dave Darrin.

Then he and Dick gazed at each other in an amazement that quickly turned in both hearts to a sickening fear.

Dave recalled the stone flying past his head; Dick remembered the flying hod of bricks. And Greg had been the third of their party who had blocked Ab. Dexter's plans!

"Oh, Greg's all right," spoke up Tom Reade cheerily.

"Then why isn't he home?" demanded Mr. Holmes. "He has had time to paddle down from Payson's three times since dark."

There was no gainsaying this statement. All five of the youngsters plainly showed their uneasiness.

"Maybe Jim Haynes knows something about the canoe," suggested Dan Dalzell.

"No; for Jim has just left our house," replied Mr. Holmes. "Jim came over to see what luck my boy had had. I'm growing more worried every minute. I think I'll go down to the river."

"We'll go with you, sir, if you don't mind," urged Dick.

"I'll be glad to have you, boys."

But the trip to the river did not lessen their worry. At the boathouse, where Jim Haynes kept his canoe, Jim's craft was the only one absent.

"There won't be any sleep in our house to-night until Greg gets home," spoke Mr. Holmes plaintively. He saw by their faces that Greg's five chums were equally uneasy. Yet all five dreaded equally to mention the bare thought that Greg might have fallen in with violence at the hands of cowardly Ab. Dexter.

"What in the wide world are we going to do?" whispered Dave aside to

Dick.

"Oh, dear, I don't really know. At any rate, we'll have to leave that to Mr. Holmes."

"Boys," spoke that gentleman suddenly, "who owns that gasoline launch yonder?"

"Mr. Edward Atwater," Dick answered.

"That looks like a powerful reflector light on the bow."

"Yes, it is, sir," Dave volunteered.

"Where does Mr. Atwater live?"

"On Benson Avenue," Tom Reade replied.

"Boys, I'm going over and see if I can induce Mr. Atwater to take us up the river to-night."

"May we go, too, sir?" begged Dick anxiously.

"Yes; if you get your parents' permission. We may be up the river late to-night."

Mr. Holmes turned on his heel, going away at a walk that was close to a run.

The five members of Dick & Co. scurried homeward. Every one of them secured permission to go with Mr. Holmes, and to be out as late as necessary. Dan Dalzell, the last of the five to get back to the boathouse, was there for some minutes ere Mr. Holmes turned up with Mr. Atwater.

The owner of the roomy launch speedily had things in running order. The "Napoleon," with the reflector light going brightly, turned out of the berth and headed up the river.

"My notion, Mr. Holmes," called the owner, sitting over the steering gear, "is that we had better go rather slowly. If you'll turn that light from side to side we ought to be able to scan the whole river as we move."

Mr. Holmes was already busy swinging the light on its pivot. Behind, peering ahead in all directions, crouched Dick Prescott and his chums.

They had gone about a mile upstream when Dick suddenly called out:

"Turn the light to the right again, Mr. Holmes, please. Yes; there it is. Don't you make out a canoe over close by the shore?"

"Turn over there, Mr. Atwater," called Mr. Holmes, his hands shaking as he tried to hold the light steadily on the floating object that Dick's keen vision had picked up.

"Is—is that Jim Haynes's canoe?" asked Mr. Holmes in a choking voice, as the launch swung in close to the drifting craft.

"Yes, sir," spoke Dick huskily. "See, there's an 'H' in a circle on the bow."

Mr. Atwater ran up so close that the boys reached over and held the canoe by its rim. There could be no doubt that it was Haynes's canoe. All of the boys recognized it.

"There are no apples in the canoe," murmured Tom Reade.

"You glutton!" muttered Dan Dalzell angrily.

"No; I wasn't thinking of that," Tom retorted indignantly. "But there being no apples shows that Greg didn't get as far as getting any. If anything happened, then it happened before he had time to load the canoe with apples."

"And that must have been hours ago," spoke Mr. Holmes with a noise in his throat that was curiously like a sob.

Silently Dick and Dave fished for the bowline of the canoe, then went back and made it fast astern.

"What now?" queried Mr. Atwater, looking at Greg's father.

"I think, perhaps, we had better go on up to Mr. Payson's," suggested Mr. Holmes. "It isn't too late to call on him, and he will be able to tell us whether Greg showed up at his house at all."

The launch was soon alongside the little landing at Mr. Payson's place. Taking a lantern from the boat, Dick and his friends explored the orchard for signs of Greg until Mr. Holmes returned.

"Mr. Payson tells me that he didn't see my boy," stated Mr. Holmes. "What can we do now, I wonder?"

"I should think, sir," Dick suggested, "that it's plain enough that Greg didn't try to go home by the river. The canoe may have gotten adrift, and he may have started toward home on foot. Some of us, I think, ought to follow the road. We may find Greg somewhere along the road, injured as a result of some accident."

"That's a good idea," nodded Mr. Holmes. "Yet I shall want Mr. Atwater to keep on searching along the river, and some of you boys ought to be with him, using your sharp eyes."

A conference was held at the landing. Tom Reade and Harry Hazelton boarded the "Napoleon," after which Mr. Holmes and the other boys set out for the road.

Truth to tell, neither those aboard the launch nor those who slowly followed the road back to Gridley had much hope of encountering news of the missing Greg.

"He has fallen in with Ab. Dexter or Driggs," whispered Dave to Dick when they were so far from Mr. Holmes that the latter could not overhear them.

"That's the way I feel about it," nodded young Prescott. "First, the affair of the bricks for mine; then the big stone that whizzed by within an inch of your head at night. And now Greg, the third of us to spoil the abduction plan, is mysteriously missing."

"There's some scoundrelly plan back of all three affairs," replied Dave Darrin with conviction. "Yet why should Dexter take all this trouble to punish boys?"

"First of all, because we interfered with him, and spoiled his bold stroke," guessed Dick Prescott. "Next, through hitting so mysteriously at us all, he probably hopes to scare Mrs. Dexter out of her life. If Dexter gets her thoroughly nervous and cowed probably she'll buy him off with a lot of her inherited money. That fellow Dexter would do anything on earth to escape the penalty of having to work for his living."

"The mean rascal!" was all Dave could mutter, and he said it with pent-up savagery.

Wherever a light showed along the country road the seekers after Greg knocked at doors. Invariably the answer was the same—no tidings.

It was after one o'clock Sunday morning when the Grammar School boys returned to their several homes, discouraged and heartsick.

Of course the "Blade" got wind of the affair and had Len Spencer and another reporter out working on the mystery.

The police, too, took a hand, though there was an absolute lack of clues upon which to work.

Broad daylight came Sunday morning, and still no Greg Holmes accounted for. Now, the police took a further hand by beginning to drag the river.

The mystery continued throughout that long, dreary day. The Grammar School boys felt as though "there had been a death in the family." Len Spencer was aware of the suspicions against Ab. Dexter, but, through fear of the libel law, he was restrained from putting his suspicions into print until there was some real proof against Dexter.

CHAPTER X

A PROBLEM IN FOOTPRINTS

Monday morning dawned bright and clear.

Yet, at 7.40, the fire alarm whistle blew "twenty-two," the signal for "no school."

Some boys heard the whistle and wondered. Dick & Co., minus Greg, who were gathered on Main Street at the time, did not wonder.

Two minutes later a series of long, loud blasts rang out, the signal to call the populace to fire headquarters.

"Just what we thought," guessed Dick, as he, Dave, Dan, Tom and Harry started on a run. "There's no school because there's to be a general hunt for Greg."

The volunteer firemen of Gridley were among the first to reach fire headquarters. The few regulars of the fire department could not leave their posts. They must be on hand in case of fires starting.

But the police, the local militia officers and a few fire-department officials were quickly gathered and ready to lead searching parties. As swiftly as could be, the fire chief detailed the leaders for the parties that were to go in the various directions.

The boys of Gridley were left to join which ever searching parties they chose.

"Which crowd shall we go with?" asked Tom Reade.

"I think we'd better go with the crowd that's going up the river road," hinted Dick. "Have the rest of you any better plan?"

No member of Dick & Co. had a better suggestion to make, so Dick's plan prevailed.

There were some twenty men in the party that went up along the river road, and more than a dozen boys. Captain Hall, of the Gridley militia company, commanded this expedition.

"Now, just as soon as we get out into the country," explained Captain Hall, as they started, "we shall do well to spread out. We can cover a wide range of ground, and yet keep within hearing of each other, so that we can signal."

The first part of the road was covered rapidly. Out in the rural part Captain Hall halted his searching party and disposed of the men and boys under his command.

The line, when it moved forward again, extended into the fields for a considerable distance on each side of the road. Everyone had a complete description of Greg's clothing and hat when he had last left home. All were instructed, also, to look for a gunny sack, or any fragments thereof, for Greg had carried such a sack with him on his expedition up the river, and this sack had not yet been found.

"Even a shred of that sack, if found, may form a most important clue," added Captain Hall impressively. "I'll keep to the road. If a searcher finds anything that he regards as a clue, let him pass the word along to me as rapidly as possible. Then we'll halt the whole line, on each side, until that clue has been investigated. Don't any of you boys—or men, either, for that matter—get any idea that he's just tramping for pleasure. There is no telling who may have the luck to find a clue that will soon lead to the end of the search. Now, forward!"

It was with a sincere good will and much straining of eyes that the hunt started. It proved to be slow work. Every now and then some seeker came across what he thought might prove a clue, and then the line halted.

Many times footprints were the cause of halting the line. One set of footprints that a man found, and on which he passed the signal, proved, when measured by Captain Hall's tape measure, to be the prints of a pair of number-ten boots.

"Greg Holmes, a thirteen-year-old boy, hadn't feet of that size," remarked the militia officer almost sharply. "We know that young Holmes wears a number four boot."

Still the line dragged on. Noon came, finding the searching party about a mile above Payson's and in wilder country. Some of the men were decidedly hungry, as were also all of the boys.

Captain Hall's whistle blew sharply, bringing in his forces.

"We never thought, of course, of provisioning this expedition," said the officer, with a smile. "Do you see that farmhouse ahead? Spread out your line again, and look for me to signal when we come up with that farmhouse. If the folks living there have any food that they will sell, I'll pay for it, and we'll halt a few minutes to stoke up for more steam."

There was a cheer at this announcement, after which the line spread out again. Ten minutes later a halt was made at the farmhouse, and the flanks of the searching party came in. The farmer's wife, it turned out, had an assortment of food that she was willing to sell at a rather good price. On this assorted stuff the searchers fed, washing it all down with glasses of milk. Then the search was taken up once more.

"We're moving about a mile an hour now," Dave called across to Dick, as the Grammar School boys, away out on the right flank, tramped through a stretch of woods. "Greg may be a hundred miles from here at this minute. Question—what day in the week shall we have the luck to come up with him?"

"We're doing the best we can," Dick called back.

"Don't pass along that old chestnut that 'angels can do no better,'" grimaced Dave.

"Well, could they?"

"I don't know. But do you expect that we'll ever find Greg, moving along in this fashion?"

"Honestly, I don't," Dick called across. "But we're following the scheme laid down by wiser and older heads than ours, and I haven't any better plan to suggest. Have you?"

"I——" began Dave, but finished with: "Hang that branch! It flew back and hit me!"

"Look where you're going," called Prescott, as he climbed over a wall. "For your information, Dave, I'll say that we're coming to a road now."

Tom Reade, on Dick's right hand, and Harry Hazelton, on Dave's left, were also jumping into the road, which they started to cross hurriedly.

"Halt!" cried Prescott, and stood like one transfixed, staring down at the ground.

"What have you found?" jeered Tom. "A gold mine?"

"Better—I believe!" cried Dick joyously. "Hustle here, fellows! No—don't crowd too close or you'll trample it out."

"What do you see?" demanded Hazelton.

"This," answered Prescott, pointing down to the ground. His chums peered, too, and made out a very distinct footprint in the soft soil of this wild, little-used road through the woods.

"There's been a horse and wagon along here, too," Dick went on excitedly. "See the fresh wheeltracks, and the marks of the horse's hoofs?"

"But only that one bootprint," objected Tom. "It doesn't seem to me that it means much."

Dick gazed reproachfully at his grouped chums, his eyes blazing with excitement in the meantime.

"Say, don't you fellows remember how Greg ripped off the lower part of his left bootheel at football practice Friday afternoon?"

"Yes," admitted Dan Dalzell. "But how does this print prove——"

"I see!" broke in Dave Darrin tremulously. "This print, at the rear end, is from the same sort of heel."

"It surely is," nodded Dick. "Dan, you wear a number-four shoe like Greg's. Come here and let me measure the length of your left shoe with this string. Sit down first."

Young Prescott took the measure with his string, then applied it to the print in the ground.

"Same length, you see," flashed Dick triumphantly. "Fellows, that's Greg Holmes's footprint! You see, the print looks old, as though it had been made a couple of days ago. Yet there's been no rain and it isn't washed away. The footprint looks just about as old as the horse's hoof mark."

"Then you think that Greg took a carriage as far as here?" demanded Tom Reade dubiously.

"He was brought here in some sort of wagon!"

"Go on and read the rest of the page to us," begged Dan Dalzell, still skeptical.

"This was as far as Dexter, or whoever had Greg, wanted to bring him in the wagon," Dick continued, still scanning the ground, while employing his hands to wave away whichever of his chums attempted to come too close. "Probably Greg was taken somewhere not far from here. He may be mighty close to us now, fellows. Let's see. The footprint points straight ahead of us."

"Why isn't there more than one print?" insisted Harry Hazelton.

"Because Greg was probably lifted, so that he wouldn't leave too much of a trail."

"Then why aren't there more prints, especially of the man or men who lifted Greg?" questioned Dave.

"The men didn't intend to leave any trail at all," replied Dick, thinking hard. "Probably the first man down from the wagon landed on that hummock of grass there." Dick moved forward. "Yes, siree! Just look here, fellows—don't crowd too close to it and blot it out. See, there isn't a sharply lined footprint here, but there's a pressing down of the grass, as if some considerable weight had been pressed upon it."

Dick now moved slowly forward, the others on his flanks.

"Here's another footprint—the right foot, but Greg's size," he sooncalled.

Not one of the Grammar School boys but felt the full force of the excitement now.

"Say!" exploded Tom Reade suddenly. "We've plumb forgotten to pass the signal along to the others in the line."

"It's too late now. They're too far ahead of us," Dick announced. "Besides, if Greg isn't far from here, and if his captors are with him, we don't want to raise too much of a racket and scare the captors away."

"I wish they'd go away, the captors, if they're around here," grinned Dalzell. "Maybe they have guns, and would be cranky enough to use 'em on us, sooner'n give Greg up."

"If you're afraid, Dan, turn around and go back," advised Dick quietly, as he moved slowly forward. "The rest of you keep a sharp lookout for more prints around here."

"Who's afraid?" snapped Dan, his grin fading.

"Here's another footprint!" called Reade, who had ranged slightly ahead of the others.

Dick was quickly at the spot.

"That was made by Greg's left shoe," Prescott swiftly declared.

"Correct," nodded Tom Reade. "Say, fellows, we are on Greg's trail!"

The enthusiasm was "catching" by this time. The little line narrowed and the Grammar School boys pressed forward, tingling with the mystery and excitement of this problem written on the face of old Mother Earth!

CHAPTER XI

DAN SEES BEARS—IN HIS MIND

In twenty minutes, studying the ground harder than any one of the five had ever scanned a problem in arithmetic, the Grammar School boys had advanced some three hundred feet. Their course had taken them into the woods on the further side of the bridle path.

"I don't see any footprints around here," half grumbled Tom Reade.

"No," Dick replied, "because the ground is hard and stony here. This isn't the place to look for prints. But we may find some other sign at any——"

"Stop right where you are!" ordered Dave excitedly.

All halted at once, gazing up the hillside, where Dave pointed.

"Fellows, there's a big rock cropping up, and do you see that hole leading into it?"

"Looks like a bear's hole," suggested Dan, with another grin.

"Cheer up!" advised Dick, smiling. "There haven't been any bears in this part of the country in a century. But come on, fellows! That place is worth looking into."

Willingly enough all trotted up the slope to the hole in the rock, though, truth to tell, all the boys were rather footsore by this time.

The hole in the wall of rock proved to be some three feet in diameter. Dick struck a match and peered in.

"This tunnel seems to go in as far as I can see with the help of the match," young Prescott announced. "Fellows, some of us will have to crawl in here and see what we can find."

"Better not," advised Dan. "Greg isn't in there. And if that hole isn't the home of a bear then it's snakes. Ugh!"

"I'll go in with you, Dick," agreed Dave. "As for Dan, you stay out —'fraidcat'!"

"No more afraid than you are!" retorted Dalzell, stung into sudden spirit. "If you rascals are going to crawl in there, then I'm going with you. Can't take 'no' for an answer."

"If Dalzell finds any wild animals in that hole he'll feel like Daniel in the lions' den," chuckled Reade.

"I wish we had something to make a torch of," grumbled Dick. "It's slow work and a lot of nuisance to be lighting two or three matches every minute."

"Do I get a chance to go in there with you?" demanded Dan.

"I don't know whether you do or not," grimaced Dick. "You're such a scared-cat that——"

"Say that again, and you don't get—this," grinned Dalzell, hauling an object out into daylight. It proved to be a pocket electric lamp.

"Oh, you jewel!" glowed Dick.

"Am I a scared-cat?" insisted Dan, returning the lamp to his pocket.

"Nothing of the sort!" Dick declared readily.

"How about you, Dave?" demanded Dan, wheeling upon his other tormentor.

"I never admired any one's courage as much as I do yours, Danny boy," laughed Darrin.

"All right, then. You can use the lamp," conceded Dalzell, bringing it forth from his pocket and handing it over to Dick.

"Let's all hurry and get in there," proposed Tom Reade.

"Nothing like it!" rejoined Dick. "Wouldn't it be fine if we all crawled in there and Dexter and Driggs really happened to be in the neighborhood? They might come along and pen us all in there! Tom, you and Harry will have to stay outside on guard—and keep your eyes wide open."

"Hazelton can keep his ears wide open," suggested Reade. "His ears are the generous, wide-open kind, anyway."

Dick had already thrown himself on his knees, and, holding the lamp ahead of him, he crawled in as fast as he could over the rough, rocky floor of the tunnel.

Dave Darrin was right behind the leader. Third in line came Dan Dalzell, who comforted himself with the thought that, if Dick and Dave encountered anything dangerous, he (Dan) would have loads of time to crawl out again before the danger could assail him.

For more than a dozen feet the tunnel ran irregularly into the rock. Suddenly Dick uttered an excited shout.

"Whh-a-at's the matter?" almost chattered Dalzell. "What's hit you?"

"There's a regular cave here," Dick called back. "A fine, big place!"

At this moment Dave, too, straightened up as he stepped into the cave proper.

"What's going on in there?" Tom Reade called in through the tunnel.

"Stay where you are," Dalzell called back, "and don't let us get bagged in here by any one."

Then Dan straightened up on his feet and took several curious looks about him while Dick flashed the light.

"Say, this is bigger'n a barn in here, only not so high!" gasped Dan.

"I wonder why nobody ever knew of this dandy place before?" mused Dave. "And the air's good in here, too."

"The air's good enough," Dick assented hurriedly. "But what we came here for was to see whether we can find Greg. Come on, fellows—be quick."

"This leads to nothing, after all," sighed Dave Darrin at last.

"There may be other parts to the cave that we haven't found yet," advanced young Prescott. "Now, halt, everyone! Quiet! Greg?"

Dick's voice echoed in the place. Away off in one corner something seemed to be stirring.

"What's that?" asked Dick quickly.

"Time to beat it!" muttered Dan. "We've disturbed some animal that lives here."

"Sh!" ordered Prescott, holding up one hand. "Greg!"

Against their ear-drums came again, rather faintly, the sound of something moving.

"If you're Greg, you keep on making the noise until I locate you," urged Dick. "Fellows, you stay right where you are. Don't move."

Once more that sound of something moving came to the boys, and Dick, on tip-toe, moving softly, ranged toward the direction from which he believed the noise had come. As Dick moved away from them with the light, Dave and Dan found themselves in comparative darkness.

"If that's you, Greg, keep on making all the noise you can," directed young Prescott, as he neared one of the jutting ledges of rock.

A distant snort came as though in answer.

"If that's you, Greg, you can do it again," cried Dick in a low, eager voice. "If it's you, do it just four times."

Then Dick halted, realizing in the stillness that he could hear his own heart beating rapidly.

Again came the snort—one, two, three—four times. Then it stopped.

"Dave! Dan!" quivered Dick's voice. "Come running! It'sGreg."

There was a sound of running feet—then a thump. Dave Darrin was still coming, but Dan had tripped over some little obstacle and had fallen flat.

"Hold on, there, you two!" howled Dan. "I've hurt my knee. Wait until I reach you."

But Dave and Dick paid no heed. Once more they had heard the snorts, and had made a dash for a low ledge of rock, from behind which they believed the sounds to have come.

Then both young leaders of the Grammar School boys gave a joyous whoop, mingled with dismay.

CHAPTER XII

THE BOY WITH THE OAKUM TASTE

"Hustle, Dan! We've found him!" rang Dave Darrin's voice, echoing through the rock-bound spaces.

"Greg, old fellow, you've had us worried," gasped Dick Prescott, sinking to the stone floor beside his friend.

Greg lay on the floor, tightly bound hand and foot, a gag of oakum stuck in his mouth and securely held there by cloth tightly strapped in place.

"Get your knife open, Dave, while I hold the light," ordered Dick. "We've got to have Greg free at once. See how white and sick he looks."

Slash! Dave cut away the gag first of all, picking out all he could of the gag.

"Ugh!" sputtered young Holmes, spitting out shreds of oakum. "You bet I'm sick!"

"How do you feel?" Dick asked anxiously, as Dave rolled Greg over and began to cut away the cords at the lad's wrists.

"Sick!" muttered Greg. "Sick of the very taste of that oakum stuff. Did you ever eat any oakum?"

"Can't say that I did," laughed Dick merrily, now that he knew at last that his chum was safe.

"You haven't missed much," growled Greg.

"There, your hands are free," announced practical Dave. "How long have you been here, Holmesy?"

"Since Saturday afternoon."

"Had anything to eat?" Dick wanted to know.

"No; and I'll have to get the taste of that vile oakum out of my mouth before I can endure the taste of food," uttered Greg dismally.

Darrin had made the last slash at Greg's foot-lashings.

"Now, get up, old fellow!"

Both helped young Holmes to his feet, but he would have fallen had not Dick caught him.

“Circulation’s all stopped,” muttered Greg disgustedly. “No wonder! The scoundrels must have tied me as tight as they knew how. Ugh! That fierce oakum taste!”

“Say, you’ll be the hero of the town when you get home, Greg,” proclaimed Dan Dalzell, who had groped his way to the spot.

“Hero? With that oakum taste in my mouth?” sputtered young Holmes. “Bosh! I’d sooner have a good gargle than be two heroes!”

While Dick supported the rescued boy, Dave Darrin was rubbing Greg’s legs roughly up and down to promote better circulation.

“Now, take a few steps,” advised Dave. “See how you can go.”

Supported by Dick’s arm, Greg did fairly well in the way of walking. Of course every step that he took helped restore the circulation.

“Wow! There’s going to be an exciting time in Gridley,” grinned Dan Dalzell.

“What day is it now?” inquired Greg.

“Monday—afternoon,” Prescott answered.

“My folks must be stirred up.”

“They’re crazy,” Dan supplied very impressively.

“How far is this place from Gridley?”

“Six miles. Don’t you know where you are, Greg!”

“Haven’t an idea in the world.”

“How did you get here? What happened?”

“Wait a little while,” begged Greg. “I’ve just got to spit all the oakum taste out of my mouth before I want to do much talking.”

By this time they were at the tunnel that led outside.

“Hullo, Tom!” called Dick through the tunnel.

“Hullo yourself, and see how you like it!” came from outside.

“Tom,” cried Dick joyously, “we’ve found Greg! We’re bringing him with us.”

“Can’t he bring himself?” demanded Reade. Then, in a suddenly scared voice:

“Is he—dead?”

"Dead sore on oakum as a food," laughed Dan, grinning broadly.

Dick, holding the light, was piloting Greg through the tunnel. In a few moments all were outside. Tom and Harry danced a jig for sheer joy.

"Greg, aren't you thirsty?" demanded Dick, as young Holmes stood blinking in the bright sunlight.

"I shall be, as soon as I get the oakum washed out of my mouth," grimaced Greg. "Whew! What a vile taste that sort of stuff has!"

"Folks in the good old town won't believe us when we get back," muttered Darrin.

"Yes, they will; they'll have to," insisted Dan, producing some articles from one of his pockets. "Here are some of the cords you cut from Greg's wrists and ankles, and here's some of the oakum."

"Throw that oakum stuff away, or else hide it. Please do," begged young Holmes, making a wry face.

"Come on. There's no time to be lost," advised Dick. "We've got a long way to go, and Greg needs the exercise. Besides, he's thirsty and hungry—or ought to be."

Within five minutes the Grammar School boys came across a spring. There Greg knelt and took in several mouthfuls, one after another, for the purpose of rinsing his mouth of that nauseating oakum taste. Then, at last, he swallowed water freely.

"My, but it's good to be out in the world again," breathed Greg happily. "But how did you fellows find me?"

"The whole town turned out to search," Dick explained. "There was no school to-day. And we came across clues that led us here. That's enough, from our side. Now, tell us how you came to be in such a fix."

At this point the Grammar School boys came out on the highway.

"Better each put a few stones in your pockets, fellows," advised Dick Prescott, stooping. "If we should meet any one we don't want to meet, stones might not prove such bad ammunition. Now, Greg, start in and tell us what happened."

"You know that big clump of bushes near the landing at Payson's?" asked young Holmes.

"Yes."

"Well, Saturday afternoon I landed, tied the canoe and then, with a gunny sack on my arm, started toward the orchard. Just as I was going by the bushes I heard a little noise. Before I could turn I was thrown flat. Then a man was on top of me, holding my nose ground into the dirt."

"Dexter? Driggs?" questioned Prescott.

"I couldn't see who it was. Next thing my own gunny sack was forced over my head. I could feel, now, that there were two men working over me. Then my hands were yanked behind me and tied. Next my feet. I forgot to say that when I was thrown I was hurled in among the bushes. Well, after I had been bound a dark cloth of some kind was passed around the sack over my eyes."

"Didn't you holler?" asked Dan, his mouth wide open.

"Yes. While the cloth was being tied tight I thought it was time to start in to yell. At the first sound a pair of hands gripped me around the throat. Whee! I thought I was being hanged, certainly! I must have been black in the face when that scoundrel let up on choking me. Well, I took the choking as a hint that I wasn't expected to make any noise. After that I was thrown on my back, but I couldn't see anything. One man, who had rather soft hands——"

"Dexter," guessed Dick.

"Most likely. Well, he sat with one hand across my throat, and I didn't think it was my time to yell, so I lay quiet. After a while I heard a wagon coming along. Then I was lifted into the wagon and a lot of old sacking was thrown over the whole length of my body. I guess it was the same sacking that you found me lying on in the cave. Then the wagon started and I had a long ride. At last we branched off into what I guess was a sort of bridle path. Not so very long after the wagon stopped and I was lifted down to my feet. I walked a little way, guided by one of the men, and then they lifted me up and carried me. Then I felt them poking me through that tunnel. After that I saw some kind of a light, dimly, through the cloths over my head, and then I was thrown down where you found me. The light was out then, and the cloths were taken off my head. Then that sickening gag was jammed into my mouth."

"Didn't you offer any kick?" inquired Dan.

"Where was the use?" sighed Greg. "I knew that men who had gone to all that trouble to bother me wouldn't waste any time listening to what I might have to say."

"Then you don't know," inquired Dick, "if Dexter and Driggs were the men?"

"They didn't speak once, from the time they grabbed me up to the time when they left me in the cave," Greg answered. "Hours after that I must have fallen asleep. I woke up to hear their voices a little way off. They were talking in whispers. I couldn't hear all that was said, but I'm certain in my own mind that the two were Dexter and Driggs."

"Did you make out anything that they were talking about?" pressed Dick.

"Here and there I caught some of it. I heard one man scolding the other about throwing bricks and shying a stone; and so that must have been what happened to you, Dick, and to you, Dave. I'm pretty sure it was Dexter who was doing the scolding. Later I heard him say it was foolish, and this carrying me off was much more to the purpose—that a thing like my being carried away would do a heap more to 'scare that woman' and make her understand that she had some one she couldn't afford to fool with. Next the other man broke in and said that lugging me away was foolish, and only a cause of trouble. But the other man broke in, with a laugh, and said he'd make 'that woman' pay handsomely to have me set free. He said she had always been a tender-hearted woman, and would spend plenty of money to save the life of a boy who had helped her. Then the two men, I judged from the sounds, left the cave. Any way, I haven't heard any sound of them since then. I——"

Here Greg stopped suddenly, clutching at a tree that he was passing.

"Fellows, I feel about all in," he remarked brokenly. "I'm awfully dizzy, too."

"You're played out, starved and all used up—that's what ails you," exclaimed Dick sympathetically. "We'll halt here and give you a chance to rest."

In five minutes Greg declared himself fit to go on again. Dave and Dick walked on either side of him, half supporting him.

"There's a house ahead, and a telephone wire running into it," said young Prescott. "We'll try to get that far, and then we'll telephone into Gridley."

That much of the trip was made, with a couple of short halts for rest. Dick went up to the front door of the farmhouse and knocked loudly. It was the farmer himself who came to the door.

"We've found the boy that all the searching parties were out looking for," Dick announced. "May we use your telephone to send the word into Gridley?"

"You sure can," rejoined the farmer. "Come this way." Then, with a side glance at young Holmes, "I guess you're him."

“Yes,” nodded Greg.

“And you hain’t had a bite to eat for a day or two?”

“No.”

“Mother,” called the farmer, leading the way into the living room, “here’s that missing youngster that there’s been all the fuss over. He’s hungry. You know what treatment that calls for.”

Dick, in the meantime, had espied the telephone and was engaged in ringing up. He called for the police station and sent the news to the chief.

“And say that I’m hitching up a team and am going to bring you all in,” added the farmer. So Prescott added that item of information.

“Hark! Hear that?” broke in Dick a minute later, while nearly all the others were talking at once. Despite the distance there came to their ears the sound of Gridley’s fire alarm whistle, sounding the recall for all searching parties.

“Now, goodness knows I’d like to offer you a lot more to eat, young man,” said the farmer’s gray-haired wife, patting Greg’s head. “But, after fasting so long you don’t want to eat too much at first. What you’ve had ought to be enough until you’ve had your drive and are at home with your own folks.”

“I feel fine, ma’am,” responded young Holmes gratefully. “I don’t know how to thank you. And I’m glad you stopped my eating too much for my own good. I’ll be all right now, when I get home.”

The farmer drove up to the door and called out. All of Greg’s friends wanted to help him outdoors, but he insisted that he could walk all by himself. Into the farm wagon piled the Grammar School boys, after having thanked the woman of the house most heartily.

“This is a lot better’n walking, after all,” murmured Greg gratefully.

Even with his late start the boys were ahead of the searchers under Captain Hall, who had heard the signal and were now returning.

“Turn down one of the side streets, will you, please?” begged Greg, as the party neared the outskirts of Gridley. “I don’t feel exactly like meeting a whole crowd.”

For, even at a distance, it could be seen that Gridley was swarming with thousands of people who had not joined the searching parties.

Thus Greg was delivered at his own home, and the other members of Dick & Co. were up on Main Street before the news had spread of young Holmes’s return.

All sensational events are dead as soon as they have been discussed for a few hours. The police authorities visited Greg at his home and questioned him, then reluctantly decided that there was not enough evidence for issuing a warrant for Abner Dexter and his man Driggs. But the news came over, from Driggs's own town, that the fellow had been dropped from the police force there.

On Tuesday morning school went on as usual, and in the afternoon the boys of the Central Grammar went at their football practice as though nothing had happened.

Before the practice game Dick called a meeting in the field, at which he and Dave Darrin were authorized to challenge the North and South Grammar Schools to a series of games.

Within the next three days both schools had been heard from, and there seemed every prospect of keen rivalry between the boys of the three schools.

Many days went along ere Dick & Co. heard again from Dexter or the latter's henchman. Yet events were shaping that were destined to mark important pages in the history of Gridley.

Except for football, in fact, things were now so quiet that Dick Prescott had not an inkling of the startling events that were ahead of him.

CHAPTER XIII

A GREAT FOOTBALL POW-WOW

"I have important news to communicate," began Old Dut dryly, after tapping the bell for the beginning of the afternoon session.

Dick and some of his friends looked up rather placidly, for they knew what the news was to be.

"All lovers of football in the Central Grammar School," continued the principal, "are requested to meet in the usual field immediately after the close of school. The purpose is to form a league and to arrange for games between the three Grammar Schools of Gridley. I will add that I am glad that so much interest in athletics is being displayed by our young men. To show my pleasure, I will add that if any of the young men in this school are so unfortunate as to incur checks this afternoon that would keep them in after school they may serve out the checks to-morrow instead. First class in geography! For the next twenty minutes the boys of this class are requested to remember that football is not geography!"

Excited as many of the youngsters were, and great as was the temptation to whisper, it happened that not a boy in the eighth grade received a check or a demerit, as it is usually called, for any form of bad conduct that afternoon. Immediately at the close of school the almost solid legion of boys of the seventh and eighth grades started on a run for the big field in which they had been practising of late.

"Now, we'll have to wait a few minutes for the fellows from the other schools," announced Dick when he had marshaled his forces in the field. "It will take them longer to get here."

"Here come some of the North Grammar boys!" called a lookout, a few minutes later. "Hi Martin is one of them."

"Welcome to the North Grammar," called Dick, as Hi Martin and two other boys made their appearance on the field. A dozen more boys from the same school could be seen straggling along in the rear by twos and threes.

"My, but you fellows have brought a mob," was Hi's greeting.

"We invited all of the fellows of the two top grades," Dick explained.

"A small, select committee would have been better," remarked Hi. "When you have too big a crowd you can't hear each other, for everyone is talking at once. So you fellows of the Central Grammar think you can play football, do you?"

"We don't know," laughed Prescott. "We want to find out."

"Huh!"

"Here come a dozen fellows from the South Grammar," announced another lookout.

"Huh! They're coming in a mob, too," uttered Martin in some disdain. "There's at least thirty in their crowd."

"Well, you Norths have brought at least fifteen," observed Dave.

"But only three of us are a committee," retorted Hi Martin. "The other fellows are just hangers on—camp followers, so to speak."

"Don't get too chesty, Hi," objected one of the outside dozen from the North Grammar.

"Don't try to give me any orders, Ben Lollard," snapped Martin. "We got all our orders from the school before we started."

"Who represents the South Grammar?" called Dick as the new comers trooped on to the field.

"Well, aren't there enough of us here?" demanded Ted Teall.

"But Martin, of the North Grammar, thinks each school ought to be represented by a committee," explained Dick.

"Committee of three," amended Hi Martin.

"Huh! That's a dude arrangement," rejoined Ted Teall.

"We have some sense of dignity at the North Grammar," snapped Hi Martin, flushing.

"And you carry it around with you all the time," jeered young Teall.

Things began to look badly for the success of the league. Many of the North Grammar boys came from rather well-to-do families, and not a few of these boys considered themselves infinitely superior to the class of boys that helped to make up the Centrals and Souths.

"Let's not have any disagreements," urged Dick coaxingly.

"Then keep these Souths in check," grumbled Hi Martin.

"Don't let the Norths get too fresh just because they have clean collars every day," advised Ted Teall.

“Fresh? It takes a South Grammar boy to be fresh,” sputtered Hi.

“Oh, does it?” sneered Ted. “Dude!”

“Mucker!” responded Hi cheerfully.

“Say, if you could only use your hands as well as you do your mouths,” sneered Ted, “ten——”

“We do,” announced Hi Martin, bounding over in front of Teall.

“Fight! Fight!” howled half a hundred boys gleefully.

Ted Teall was more than willing, and Hi looked as though he were afraid only of soiling his hands in touching a South Grammar boy. Dick, however, darted in between the pair, and Darrin, Reade and Dalzell followed.

“Now, stop all this fooling, fellows,” begged Dick. “We all know that Ted and Hi can fight. What we want to find out is whether there are brains and muscle enough in town to get three football elevens together. Ted, put your hands in your pockets. Hi, you move back. We don’t want any fighting here.”

“Then that cub will have to stop calling names,” retorted Teall.

“You started it yourself,” retorted Martin.

“You’re another!”

“Fight! Fight!” yelled many of the young onlookers.

Ted was willing, and Martin not unwilling. Crowds surged forward, threatening to push the North and South champions to close quarters.

“Let’s go home, if nobody ain’t going to do nuthing,” remarked one South disgustedly.

“Stop all this, fellows—please do,” begged Dick once more. “Ted and Hi, you two show your good sense by shaking hands.”

“Shake hands with that?” demanded Hi scornfully, glaring at Teall.

“Shake hands with a high-collared dude?” muttered Ted. “I’d get mobbed for disgracing my part of the town.”

“You are a disgrace, anyway,” snapped back Hi.

“Now, you get back, Martin, and let us get down to real football,” directed Darrin, pushing Martin back several feet. “No; you needn’t glare at me. I won’t fight you, at all events, until the football season is over.”

Dalzell was backing up Dave in an effort to keep Martin back. Reade and Hazelton now placed themselves in front of young Teall.

"Now, come to order, please!" called Dick.

"Hey, Prescott! Who asked you to preside?" hailed a South Grammar boy.

"I don't know that I want to, either," Prescott answered, with a smile. "But some one has to start the meeting. As soon as you come to order you can choose any one you want for presiding officer. All I'm trying to do is to get the thing started. Come to order, please."

"I'll meet you on Main Street any Saturday you like, Hi Martin!" called Ted belligerently.

"I wouldn't go out of my way to meet anything like you," shot back Martin.

"Order! Order!" insisted Dick. "Come to order, fellows!"

By the aid of his chums and a few other friends, and a great deal of "sh! sh!" all through the crowd, Dick at last got the meeting into a semblance of quiet.

"Now, as I said before," Prescott went on, "all the reason I had for taking the chair——"

"Where is it?"

"What did you take it for?"

"——was to get the meeting started," Dick went on. "Now that we're at least as quiet as some of the very small boys here will allow us to be, suppose you nominate some one to preside over this meeting."

"Dick Prescott is good enough for us," sang out several Central Grammar boys.

"Hi Martin!" came from the North squad.

"Ted Teall!" insisted the South boys.

"Well, whom do you want?" insisted Dick patiently.

"Dick Prescott!" "Hi Martin!" "Ted Teall!"

"Don't waste time trying to choose a chairman, Dick," advised Dave. "Just hold on to the job yourself, and try to get something through the meeting."

But a clamor went up on all sides that lasted fully a minute.

"Mr. Chairman!" shouted Tom Reade as soon as quiet came.

"Reade," acknowledged Prescott, with a bow in Tom's direction.

"Will you kindly state the object of the meeting?"

“The object of the meeting,” Prescott went on, “is to see whether each of the three Grammar Schools in this town is able and willing to organize a football team. The object, further, is to see whether we can form the three teams into a league and play off a series of games for the championship this fall.”

“Who’s going to run the league?” demanded Ted Teall.

“That’s for this meeting to decide,” Dick answered. “I would suggest that each school nominate a committee of three to represent it in a council of nine made up from the three schools. That the council choose a chairman and that the council have full charge of league arrangements.”

“Is Hi Martin going to be in that council?” called a South boy.

“I presume so, fellows,” responded the chair. “Martin is already a member of a committee of three chosen at the North Grammar.”

“But we haven’t any committee of three,” objected a Central boy.

“We can soon straighten that out,” piped up Tom Reade. “I’m going to make a motion, and it’s addressed only to the fellows of the Central Grammar. I move that Dick Prescott, Dave Darrin and Greg Holmes represent the Central.”

“All in favor say ‘aye,’” directed Prescott.

The motion was carried with a rush, there being no dissenting voices.

“I would now suggest,” Dick continued, “that the South Grammar fellows put forward their committee of three. Then the council can get together, and soon be able to report back to the whole crowd.”

But Ted Teall, who had been talking rapidly in undertones to several of the Souths, now yelled back:

“No, sir-ree! That doesn’t go. South Grammar wants the whole thing put through in town-meeting style. Let every fellow here have his say.”

“Will that be agreeable to the North Grammar?” asked Dick, glancing at Martin.

“Not much,” retorted Hi. “South Grammar has twice as many fellows here as we have, and Central has a bigger crowd present than both other schools put together. Let’s have committees and organize ‘em into a council.”

“We Souths won’t stand for anything but town-meeting style,” bawled Ted Teall.

“But we haven’t enough fellows for that,” objected Hi strenuously.

"Why didn't you bring more?" jeered Ted. "Did the rest of your fellows have to go home to put on clean collars and practise on the piano?"

"We shan't get anywhere unless the Souths put forward a more gentlemanly fellow to speak for them," remarked Hi with stiff dignity.

"Fight!" yelled one boy hopefully.

The surging and pushing began all over again, but Dick managed to make his voice carry over the hubbub.

"Fellows, what ails you all?" he cried. "Are we going to have it said that the Grammar School fellows of Gridley haven't brains and manners enough to get together and discuss an ordinary question or two?"

"What about uniforms?" spoke up a member of Hi's committee.

"Central hopes to have uniforms," replied Dick.

"North Grammar is going to have uniforms," shouted Hi Martin, "and we want to make it plain, right now, that we won't play with any team that isn't uniformed."

This cast a damper on the Souths, who knew, to a boy, that they couldn't hope to raise money enough to buy football uniforms.

"Aw," retorted Ted Teall scornfully, "what's the use of playing football with dudes that don't dare go on to the field if they haven't nifty uniforms and clean collars?"

"That's our stand," retorted Hi with intense dignity. "North Grammar will play no un-uniformed teams."

"And South Grammar won't play any dudes," shouted Ted defiantly. "We want real meat to play against—no mush!"

"Let's hear what Central Grammar proposes on this question?" put in Hi Martin hopefully. "Prescott, you said your school would be uniformed."

"Let's go home, fellows," proposed Ted, turning away and stalking off. For a moment the other Souths hesitated. Then, with a yell, they started off after their leader.

"Good riddance to muckers!" shouted a North boy derisively.

"Come to order, please," begged Dick. "Any one who calls names is out of order. It's bad practice."

"Who asked you to run this meeting, anyway, Dick Prescott?" snapped Martin.

“No one in particular, and I’m willing you should preside if you want to, Martin.”

“The Centrals ain’t any better stuff than the Souths,” observed one of the Norths slightingly.

“Cut that out!” cried Dave, his eyes flashing. He stepped forward, looking for the fellow who had made the remark.

“I call upon the North Grammar delegation to step aside and confer for a few minutes,” announced Hi. He led his own schoolmates some two hundred feet away.

“Say, the whole scheme’s gone to pieces,” grumbled Tom Reade disgustedly.

“Wait, and we’ll see,” answered Prescott hopefully.

The North Grammar boys talked matters over among themselves for two or three minutes.

“There, see!” grumbled Greg. “Hi Martin is leading his crowd away. They’re all quitters!”

“That always seems to be the way with Grammar School fellows,” sighed Dick. “High School fellows do big things, but you can’t ever get Grammar School boys to stick together long enough to do anything!”

So Grammar School football died an almost painless death.

CHAPTER XIV

DICK STEPS INTO A DEATH-TRAP

"Hullo, Dave!"

"Hullo, Dick. I've been looking for you. My, but you're dressed up to-night. Going to a party that I haven't heard about?"

"Not exactly," laughed Dick. "I'm going to call on Mrs. Dexter."

"Oho!"

"She sent a note that she'd like to have me call this evening. What it's about I don't know."

"Then I can guess," offeredDave.

"What?"

"Mrs. Dexter was set on getting football uniforms for us. When the league dropped out at the bottom that spoiled her chance. Mrs. Dexter feels that she's under obligations, and so has sent for you in order to find what she can do in the place of buying uniforms."

"Do you think that's it?" questioned young Prescott, looking bothered.

"I'm sure of it."

"Then I wish I weren't going up there to-night."

"Have you got to?" asked Darrin.

"It would hardly look polite if I didn't go. But I'll tell you what, Dave."

"What?"

"You come along with me."

"Not much!"

"Why not?"

"First place, I'm not invited. Second place, I'm not dressed up, and you are. Extra, I don't want to look as though I were trotting up there after a reward."

"I'm not, either," Dick retorted with considerable spirit.

"I know you're not, but you can say 'no' for both of us, and for Greg thrown in."

"Then you won't come with me?"

"I'll feel more comfortable down here on Main Street," laughed Dave. "If you get back early enough you can tell me about it."

"If Mrs. Dexter doesn't want anything except to talk about rewarding us," grunted Prescott, "I can promise you that I'll be back bright and early."

"So long, then, and good luck!"

"What?"

"Good luck in getting away, I mean."

So Dick pursued his course alone, and feeling a good deal more uncomfortable, now that he had a suspicion of Mrs. Dexter's business.

Up at the pretty little Dexter cottage things had been moving serenely of late. Ab. Dexter had not been heard from, and his wife imagined that the fellow had gone to other parts. For weeks she had kept a special policeman in the house at night. On this particular evening the man wanted to be away at a lodge meeting, and Mrs. Dexter had felt that it was wholly safe to let him go, more especially, as resourceful Dick Prescott would put in part of the evening there.

When the bell rang, Jane being upstairs with little Myra, Mrs. Dexter herself opened the front door.

Then she sprang back suddenly, stifling a dismayed little scream, for Abner Dexter stood facing her.

"Didn't expect me, did you?" jeered the fellow, pushing his way into the hall. "Jennie, I'm at the end of my rope, and of my patience, too. I'm broke—have hardly a dollar in the world, and now you've got to do your duty and provide for me in the way that a rich wife should. In there withyou!"

Ab. pushed her into a little room just beyond the parlor, and stepped in after her.

"Nice, comfortable place you have here, while I'm wondering where my next meal is coming from!" sneered the fellow.

"Abner, I gave you ten thousand dollars, and you promised to leave me alone," protested the woman, afraid of the evil look that she now saw in her worthless husband's face.

"Well, I haven't any of that money, and I've got to have more," retorted Dexter emphatically. "Jennie, I want twenty-five thousand dollars. Give me that, and I'll leave the country for good."

"I—I couldn't trust you," shefaltered.

"Don't talk that way to me!"

"I have good reason to, Abner, and you know it."

"You thought I had forgotten you, didn't you?" he sneered harshly.

"I hoped that you had at last made up your mind to let me alone," replied the woman, trying to summon a bravery that she did not feel.

"I haven't forgotten you. Jennie, you will have to find and turn over to me the twenty-five thousand dollars that I want. You will never know any peace until you do do it, and you will never see me again after you have given me the money. Now, aren't you going to be sensible?"

"Yes," she flashed. "I'm going to be too sensible to listen to you any longer. You have been watching this house, and you came to-night because you knew I was alone. If you won't go, at least I shall not stay here to listen to you."

"Oh, yes, you will," replied the man angrily, barring the doorway.

At that instant the telephone bell in a niche in the hallway sounded.

"Let me answer that call," cried Mrs. Dexter.

"No, I won't!"

Then both heard, with very different feelings, a voice speaking these words:

"Central, I am Dick Prescott, at Mrs. Dexter's. I shall probably be interfered with. Call up the police station in a hurry and say that Dexter is here, threatening Mrs. Dexter, who is without defense. I——"

Slam! Dick felt himself seized by the collar. He was banged up roughly against the wall.

"You young hound!" blazed Ab. Dexter.

"Don't hurt him!" screamed Mrs. Dexter.

"I'll do as I please with this young hound!" snarled Dexter hoarsely. "What right has he interfering with me in this manner? Come along, you meddling youngster!"

As the telephone connection was still open, the girl at central office was able to hear every word.

Ab. Dexter, still gripping struggling Prescott by the collar, dragged him down the hallway and into the same room where he had recently been talking with his unfortunate wife. Mrs. Dexter followed, pleading.

"What are you doing here?" blazed Dexter, giving Dick a shaking that made his teeth rattle.

"I sent for him, Abner. I wanted to find how I could best reward him for ——"

"For interfering with me on another occasion—yes, I know!" finished her husband, glaring at her. "You'd spend a lot of money on any one who tried to injure me, but you wouldn't give me a cent to keep me from starving!"

As Dexter rattled off this charge he worked himself up into a passion. He shook Dick again, until he espied a closet in the room, in the lock of which was the key.

"In there for you!" snarled Dexter, still shaking Prescott and dragging him across the room. Slam! Into the closet went Dick. Click! went the lock, and Dexter thrust the key into his pocket.

"I'll take command of things here, as I ought to," growled the man. "As for you, Jennie, here's another closet on the other side of the room. Come, for I don't want to hurt you."

Frightened badly now, the woman obeyed the impulse of Dexter's hand on her arm. She sank, cowering, into the other closet. Dexter turned the key in that lock also.

"Now, are you going to come to your senses?" He called through the locked door to his wife.

"If you mean am I going to give you any more money, I am not!" came Mrs. Dexter's reply, in a firmer tone, for she had been stung anew into defiance.

"Then good night—and good-bye!" he laughed harshly.

Both captives heard the scratching of a match. Dexter held the small flame against a drapery until it was burning freely.

He had no intention of having his wife burn up in the house, for, dead, her money would be lost to him forever. He planned only to scare her into nervous collapse. But Jane, the housekeeper, did not liberate the captives in the two closets as Dexter had expected. Instead, as the housekeeper came to the head of the stairs, heard the crackling of flames and smelled the rising smoke, she fell on the landing in a faint.

"Dick! Dick!" screamed Mrs. Dexter's voice. "The house is afire. Can't you break down the door and save us both?"

“I’m trying to,” shouted back young Prescott above the din of his own blows. “I’m trying to—but I’m afraid this door is too strong for me!”

CHAPTER XV

WHAT GRAMMAR SCHOOL BOYS CAN DO

Inside of a minute Dick Prescott was both gasping and despairing.

Outside the volume of smoke was increasing. Some of it worked in through the cracks around the door.

Coughing, choking, trembling in a cold chill of dread, Dick continued frantically to hurl himself against the door.

"Can't you get out, Dick?"

"I'm awfully afraid I can't."

"Nor can I," screamed back Mrs. Dexter, though she was doing nothing besides beating a feeble tattoo with her soft fists against the panels of the door of her prison. "Jane! Jane!"

But the housekeeper still lay in a death-like faint above. As for Myra, she slept as only a tired small child can sleep.

"Oh, Dick, you must break down your door!" screamed the woman. "Myra —my child—upstairs. She'll be burned to death!"

"I'll keep on trying, ma'am, as long as I have any life left," Dick promised, chokingly.

Brave words! Young as he was, Dick Prescott was not of the kind to die a coward's death. Yet, in his own mind he was convinced that the door was too stout for him.

"You can't save us, can you?" called Mrs. Dexter's own choking tones finally.

"I'm still trying, ma'am."

"But you don't expect to succeed. Tell me the truth."

"I shan't give up, ma'am, but I am afraid that all the chances are against us!"

Bang! Bang! went Dick's shoulders against the panels. He was aching now from his hopeless exertions.

Yet, every time that he paused he heard the crackling of the flames outside. The sound told him that the woodwork had caught at last.

"Dick!"

"Yes, ma'am."

"I'm quite calm now."

"I'm glad to hear that, Mrs. Dexter."

"I've stopped thinking of myself, Dick. I know that my little Myra is asleep. She'll suffocate, and won't wake up to know any pain."

"But where's your housekeeper?"

"She must have slipped out after she put Myra to bed. There's no hope for us, Dick. We must go as bravely as we can. But, my poor boy, I can't tell you how sorry I am that helping me has brought you to such a plight."

"But you forget, Mrs. Dexter. Central will send a policeman. He will find out what's wrong here and save us."

"Don't try to comfort me with false hopes, Dick. You and I both know that the policeman can't get here in time to save us."

This had, indeed, occurred to Dick some moments before, but he wanted to help Mrs. Dexter to keep her courage up as long as possible.

"Dick," called a subdued voice, "your mother taught you to pray?"

"Oh, yes, ma'am."

"Then you know how to pray now—the last chance you'll have."

"All right, then," young Prescott shot back to her, "and I'll keep on working while I pray!"

Mrs. Dexter did not speak again. The smoke, passing into the closet, had proved too much for her, and she had collapsed on the floor.

But Dick, naturally stronger, and with robust lungs, was still fighting bravely, though he was conscious that he was growing feebler and that air was harder to get.

Then there came to his ears two sounds of the sweetest description. The first noise was that of running feet. The second was Dave Darrin's voice shouting:

"Fellows, there's some fearful work going on here. And here's the fire! Move like lightning! Bring water from the kitchen—in anything."

There was a sound of many running feet. Then Dick called, huskily:

"Dave, are you there?"

"Dick, where are you?"

"In this closet—locked in!"

"But there doesn't seem to be any key," quivered Darrin.

"No; Dexter took that away with him."

"Did he set this——"

"Yes; but listen! Mrs. Dexter is locked up in the closet opposite."

Dave crossed the room in a flash. Finding the key in the lock of the other closet door, Dave Darrin turned it and found Mrs. Dexter lying on the floor.

"Fellows!" bawled Dave hoarsely. "Never mind the water. Come here—on the jump!"

Half a dozen boys ran back into the room, just in time to see Dave struggling to drag Mrs. Dexter out to the front porch.

"One of you help me," directed Darrin. "The others batter down that closet door over there. Dick Prescott is locked up there, and there is no key."

"Here's a hatchet," cried another boy, running in from the kitchen. "Clear the way and let me at the door."

The boy was Greg Holmes. He brought the hatchet down with telling force at each blow, smashing all the paneling around the lock. In a very few moments Greg had the door open, and he and Dave helped catch Dick as the latter fell forward, dizzy and all but unconscious.

"Rush him out on to the front porch!" ordered Dave. "Then we'll come back and fight the fire!"

"Has—has anyone turned in an alarm?" inquired Dick, as he reached the porch and took in a life-saving breath of the pure, cool air.

"No," admitted Dave. "We forgot that. But I'll run and do it now."

"What's the matter? Fire?" called a man from the next yard.

"Yes," Dave yelled back. "Run and turn in an alarm, won't you?"

"I surely will," came the answer.

This left Dave free to remain and do what he could.

"I'm all right now," declared Dick, getting up out of the chair into which he had been dropped, though he was not yet any too strong. "Dave, you and the other fellows fight the fire the best you can. Greg, you come upstairs with me, and we'll find Myra and get her out of the smoke."

At the head of the stairs Prescott and Holmes found Jane, still in a faint.

"We'll need more help to get her downstairs," muttered Dick. "Greg, you find Myra, bundle her in blankets and rush down with her. I'll stay here until you come back."

When Greg, after darting downstairs with the child, returned, he had two other boys with him. It took all four to get Jane down and outside to one of the porch chairs.

"This is work for the doctor," announced Dick, looking from Jane to Mrs. Dexter. "You other fellows jump in to get the fire out, and I'll 'phone for Dr. Bentley. He's Mrs. Dexter's doctor."

While making that comment, Dick darted back to the telephone. As seconds were precious here, he merely called up central and stated what was wanted. Then he ran to join the others.

"There's a hose outside this window. I've seen it before," called Prescott, opening the window and jumping outside. Then:

"Dave!"

"Here I am, Dick."

"Here's the hose. I'll pass the nozzle in and then turn the water on."

"Bully for you, Handy Andy!"

Sizz-zz! Dave directed the stream against the liveliest flames. It was only a lawn-sprinkling hose that he held, but even that threw a lot of water.

Dick climbed in through the window again.

"We'll hold things down until the firemen get here," he announced energetically.

So busy had all been that only two or three out of the ten boys present had noticed that the fire-alarm whistle had called off the box number some time previously.

Finally, with a screeching of whistles and a clanging of gongs, a part of the Gridley Fire Department hauled up outside.

While hosemen fastened a line to a hydrant, and nozzlemen dragged the lengths in through the wide-open front door, the chief ran ahead of them.

"Where's the fire?" he called, and made his way inside.

"Well, you boys are dandies!" remarked the chief grimly. Then he ran out to the front door.

"Shut that stream off!" the chief bellowed hoarsely. "A lot of Grammar School boys have put the fire out with a lawn hose."

Two or three minutes later the policeman whom Prescott had summoned arrived, out of breath. Two minutes after that Dr. Bentley's auto stopped at the door.

Both unconscious women were revived, and Myra, who had not once awakened in all the excitement, was taken up and tucked in bed.

"How did you get into the house, Dick?" Mrs. Dexter at last found time to inquire.

"Why, the door was open just a crack, ma'am, when I got here. I heard Dexter threatening you, and realized that you must be alone. I knew I couldn't do much alone, so I sneaked in as softly as I could and got to the telephone."

As soon as he found himself with only his boy friends about, Dick demanded to know how they had arrived so opportunely.

"That's easy enough," Dave Darrin explained. "Just after you left me I ran into Greg, Tom, Dan and Harry. I told them where you'd gone, and what the business would probably turn out to be. Then—then—well, we got so awfully curious that we made up our minds to stroll up here to the corner and wait until you came out. Then we ran into four other fellows from our school, and there was a mob of us. To kill time we walked down past. As we went past we saw smoke coming out of one of the open windows on the ground floor. Then Bert Johnson remembered that he had seen Ab. Dexter come out and hurry away. It didn't take us long, then, to make up our minds to get into the house. We found the front door unlocked, and the rest was easy."

"We'll get out of here as soon as we can now," hinted Dick.

"Why?" Dalzell wanted to know, "This is the center of all the excitement in town to-night."

"Yes," Prescott replied, "but as soon as Mrs. Dexter thinks of it she'll send for us and offer more thanks and rewards. We can get away 'most any time now. And there comes her special policeman. Dexter won't be back to-night, anyway."

So the Grammar School boys slipped away, but they had added another page to the history of Gridley.

Dexter, with his usual luck, appeared to have made a safe retreat. The police paid a visit to his former cave up the road, but did not catch him there, although a police guard was kept at the cave for three days.

But Dick received a postal card, on the back of which was printed:

"If you ever interfere with me again, I promise you that your luck is at an end!"

The message was unsigned, but the message was postmarked at Gridley.

CHAPTER XVI

OUT FOR HALLOWE'EN FUN

"There'll be loads of fun to-night," proclaimed Dan Dalzell, his eyes sparkling with mischief, as he danced up and down in the schoolyard at forenoon recess.

"Why?" asked Dick innocently.

"Don't you know what day this is?" Dan insisted.

"Yes; and I also know that to-night will be Hallowe'en."

"Then don't you know that there are going to be several barrels of fun uncorked in this old burg to-night?"

"I didn't know that barrels were ever 'uncorked,'" replied Dick judicially.

"Oh, pshaw! This isn't the first class in language!" retorted Dan disdainfully. "You're going to be out to see the fun, aren't you?"

"I suppose likely I shall be out on the street a little while after supper," Prescott admitted.

"Hear the young saint!" taunted Dan derisively, appealing to a group of boys. "No one would ever suppose that Dick Prescott had ever gotten up any mischief—hey?"

"Oh, Dick will have one or two tricks ready for us to trim our enemies with to-night," replied Ben Alvord. "Don't worry!"

"Sure! Dick never yet went back on the crowd," declared Wrecker Lane. "He's got a few good ones ready right now."

"Have you, Dick?" demanded a chorus of eager voices.

"Tell us one or two of the tricks now," pressed "Hoof" Sadby.

But Dick shook his head.

"Come on out with it!" coaxed Spoff Henderson.

"Ain't he the mean one—keeping it all to himself?"

"If Dick has anything hidden in his sleeve," broke in Tom Reade, "he'd show a lot of sense, wouldn't he, telling it to a lot of you fellows with loose-jointed tongues? Why, it would be in the evening paper, and the folks we want to torment would be at their gates waiting for us."

"We won't tell—won't breathe a word! Honest!" came in instant denial.

"I'll tell you just one thing, fellows, if you think you really can keep it to yourselves," grinned Dick.

"Go ahead!"

"Don't trust these talkative Indians with anything in advance, Dick," protested Tom Reade.

"Yes, yes—go ahead!" cried the boys.

"You won't tell, fellows, will you?" Dick fenced.

"Cross our hearts we won't."

"Well, then, fellows, the truth is that you are all on the wrong scent. I haven't thought up a blessed prank for to-night."

"Aw!" came an unbelieving chorus.

"Let's make him tell. Get hold of him. We'll paddle Dick Prescott until he'll be glad to tell."

There was a rush, but Dave and Tom got in front of Dick.

"Who wants to try the paddle first?" asked Dave, his fists clenching, as he faced the mischievous Grammar School boys.

"But I haven't thought of a thing, fellows," protested Prescott.

"Say, I want some of you fellows to help me take off old Pond's gate to-night," called Toby Ross. "We can take it down and hang it on the fountain in the square. That'll be a good mile from his house, and old Pond will be awful mad, because he'll have to tote it all the way back himself. He's too stingy to hire a teamster to take it back."

"And that's your idea of fun is it?" demanded Dick.

"Sure!" grinned Toby.

"It might be for a seven-year-old, but it sounds pretty stupid for an eighth grader."

"What do you want me to do, then—set old Pond's house a-fire?" queried Toby with an injured air.

"We'll have to take down a lot of signs and change 'em," proposed Ned Allen.

"What do you think of that, Dick?" asked Spoff Henderson.

"That sounds kiddish, too, doesn't it?" objected Dick. "And the trick is at least three times as old as Gridley."

"We can slip in at the back of George Farmer's place," suggested Wrecker Lane. "You know, he's always bragging about the fine milk he serves. Well, if we can get in at the cooling trough in his yard we can empty half the milk out of each big can and fill it up with water. Then won't he hear a row from his customers about watered milk?"

That brought a guffaw from some of the youngsters, but Dick shook his head.

"That's kiddish, too," he remarked.

"Say, what do you call kiddish tricks?" Hoof Sadby wanted to know.

"Why, things that have been done, over and over again, by small boys. All the tricks you fellows have named have been done by our grandfathers. That's why I call 'em kiddish. A fellow who can't think up a new one is only a kid. Use your brains, fellows."

"Well, if you're so all-fired smart, you tell us a new one that has some ginger in it," growled Wrecker.

"I told you that I hadn't any," retorted Dick. "I admit that I'm dull. But, if I do play any tricks to-night, they'll have to be just a little bit new. Boys of our age haven't any business traveling around with Hallowe'en jokes that are so old that they've voted and worn whiskers for forty years. It isn't showing proper respect for old age."

"Dick has a few new ones in his tank. Don't you worry about that," muttered some of the wise ones. "You just find Dick & Co. on the street to-night, and stick to 'em, and you'll see plenty of fun happening."

"I'll tell you something else that we fellows are growing a bit too old for, too, if you want to know," Dick offered presently, for the crowd still insisted on hanging out close to this usually fertile leader in fun.

"Fire away," groaned Spoff.

"Well, then, I mean the kind of tricks that destroy people's property. The fellow that shies a stone through the window of some one he doesn't like, or who carries off gates, or tramples flower beds is only a cheap penny pirate."

That was rather daring, for Dick's condemnation had touched rather closely some forms of mischief that boys always imagine as belonging to them on Hallowe'en night.

However, the general opinion was against quarreling with Dick. Without him and his chums on the streets, the Grammar School boys knew that there wouldn't be as much sport.

"You're trying to think up some good ones, aren't you?" asked Dave, as he and Dick were about to part on the homeward way at noon.

"Yes, of course; but I hope you other fellows have brains that are working faster than mine is to-day."

"Oh, you'll have something ready by to-night," laughed Dave.

"I hope so."

That afternoon the boys and girls in Old Dut's room did not appear to have their minds very much on their lessons. A man of Old Dut's experience knew why.

"I'll stay at home and sit tight on my place to-night," murmured the principal to himself. "Like as not I'm slated to be one of the biggest Hallowe'en victims."

When Dick reached Main Street that evening he found himself instantly the center of a crowd of at least twenty boys from the Central Grammar.

"What'll we do, Dick?" came the hail.

"Anything you like," agreed Prescott.

"But what have you thought up?"

"Nothing."

"Cut that!"

"Honest, fellows, I haven't."

"Never mind," sang out Dave. "We fellows will just roam around town for a while and see what is happening. Something will pop into our minds, and then we can have a bit of mischief."

"Hullo!" muttered Toby. "Say! Just look at Hoof!"

"Whatcher got there, Hoof?" demanded a laughing chorus.

For Hoof Sadby, looking more sheepish than ever before in his life, had appeared on the scene carrying a baby. It was a real, live one, too—his year-and-a-half-old brother, to be exact.

"Say, don't guy me too much, fellows," begged Hoof sadly. "I'm in a pickle, sure. Pop and mother are going to a sociable to-night. That is, they've already gone. And they said——" Hoof paused. "They said——" he tried again. Then, in final desperation he shot it out quickly. "They said I'd have to stay home, and—mind the baby!"

"Isn't that a shame?" came a sympathetic chorus, but a few of the fellows laughed.

"It's a boy, any way," argued Hoof, rather brokenly, "and a smart little fellow, too. Now, if he's going to grow up right as a boy the kid ought to start in early. So I've wrapped him up warm and have brought him out with me."

"What are you going to do with him, Hoof?"

"I'm going to tote the little fellow around to see the fun—if you fellows can stand having me with you," announced Hoof sadly, rather pleadingly.

"Why, of course you can come, can't he, fellows?" appealed Dick.

"If you're sure that the youngster won't catch cold," agreed Tom Reade. "A baby is a human being, you know, and has some rights of his own."

"Oh, I won't let the little shaver catch cold," promised Hoof. "See how warmly I've got him wrapped up."

As some of the fellows crowded about their encumbered mate, baby laughed and tried to reach them.

"He's a good fellow, if he is young," spoke up Greg. "Bring him along, Hoof."

So that was settled, and the crowd turned down one of the side streets. These darker thoroughfares, as all knew by experience, were safer for Hallowe'en pranks. The dark places were the easiest ones in which to escape when pursuit offered.

Nor had the Grammar School crowd been strolling along more than two minutes when Dick suddenly halted them by holding up one hand.

"What is it?" whispered several, mysteriously, as they crowded about the leader.

"There's Mose Waterman's house, and it's all dark there," murmured Dick. "And it's the same over at Mr. Gordon's. Now, you know, Waterman and Gordon have never spoken to each other since they had that law suit."

"Yes, yes!"

"Well, the warm weather lately has led Mose Waterman to leave his porch chairs out later'n usual. Now, fellows, suppose we lift the chairs from Waterman's porch and put 'em over on Gordon's porch. That wouldn't be far for Waterman to go after 'em, but do you think he'd do it? Never! He will growl, and swear that Gordon stole the chairs. And Mr. Gordon is too angry with Mose Waterman to take the chairs back. So it'll give us fun for a fortnight strolling by in the day time and noticing whether Waterman has his chairs back."

"Wow!" "Whoop!" "And you said, Dick"—reproachfully—"that you couldn't think up anything!"

Half a dozen figures moved swiftly and stealthily. In a twinkling the transfer of porch chairs from Waterman's house to Gordon's had been made. The young mischief-makers passed on, looking for more nonsense. But that joke became almost classic in Gridley. For days and days after that Waterman and Gordon glared at each other from their front windows, or whenever they met on the street. But neither would touch the chairs, and neighbors grinned every time they passed and saw the chairs still on the Gordon porch. One night, in November, however, Gordon took the chairs as far as the middle of the road. An hour later Mose Waterman slipped out from his unlighted house and carried the chairs back and into his own house. The neighbors had had their hearty laughs, however.

"Say, I'll bet that's the best thing done to-night," chuckled Toby Ross, as the "gang" pressed on to new scenes and new laughs.

But it wasn't quite the best thing done that night as later events showed.

CHAPTER XVII

THE NEWEST TRICK OF ALL

"Here's where old Miss Lowthry lives," muttered Ned Allen, halting before a gate leading into the grounds surrounding a cosy littlecottage.

"It wouldn't be very manly to do anything to scare lone women, would it?" demanded Dick.

"She's an old maid," protested Toby.

"That's no crime," insisted Dick.

"She has no use for boys," breathed Ben Alvord, complainingly.

"From some things that boys do, I don't altogether blame her," chuckled young Prescott.

"And—say! Don't Miss Lowthry hate babies!" grunted Wrecker Lane. "You remember Fred Porter? His folks used to live in that next house. When Fred was a baby they say he used to cry something awful. Well, once in the summer, after Fred had cried every night for a week, and Miss Lowthry had to hear it all through her open windows, what did she do but go to the health board and ask that the Porters be ordered to make their baby stop crying. There was an awful fuss about it, and Miss Lowthry made some talk about all babies being brats."

"They are not," denied Hoof Sadby indignantly.

"That's what I'm trying to tell you," went on Wrecker calmly. "That's why I have no use for old maids that hate babies. Now, there are some old maids that are really fine. But Miss Lowthry!"

"Wrecker, you live right near here," murmured Dick suddenly.

"'Course I do."

"Then come aside. I want to whisper something to you."

Then Dick talked in whispers with Wrecker for a few moments. The other boy was seen by the curious suddenly to double up with laughter. From that attitude Wrecker recovered, only to start off on the run.

"Say, what is it?" demanded a dozen cautious voices as Dick came back to the crowd.

"Now, see here, fellows, don't want to know too much. Just stay around and see what happens, and you'll all enjoy it as much as Miss Lowthry does."

"Then it's against her?" breathed Ben Alvord. "Good! great!"

"Now, you, Dave, stay here with me," Dick went on, disposing of his forces with the air of a general. "The rest of you fellows scoot across the lawn and hide in the bushes. Hide so that you can't be seen from the street or from the front door of the cottage, either. Then just wait and see what happens."

Tom Reade and Greg managed to get the crowd started. Then Dick called, softly:

"Oh, say, Hoof! I'll hold the baby for you a while. You must be tired."

Hoof started, and glared suspiciously. But he knew that Dick was "always on the square," and so, after swallowing hard, passed the tiny, bundled youngster over to Prescott's waiting arms. "Say, be careful what you do with him," pleaded Sadby. "He's a fine little fellow."

Then the crowd hid. How they watched and waited! Miss Lowthry's sitting room was lighted, and the boys could see her, seated in a rocking chair, reading a book.

It seemed ages ere Wrecker Lane returned. When he came he brought a basket. Some soft fragments of blanket rested in the bottom of it.

"Just the thing," chuckled Dick softly, placing the baby in the basket. "Now, skip over there, Wrecker, and hide with the fellows in the bushes."

Dick waited until Wrecker Lane vanished.

"Now, come along, Dave," chuckled Prescott. "You ring the bell just as I place the basket on the steps. Then we'll both hot-foot it to join the fellows."

A few moments later Dick and Dave scurried to cover, snuggling down among a lot of Grammar School boys who were holding their handkerchiefs wedged in their mouths.

Then they heard the front door open, saw Miss Lowthry peer out, and then heard her utter a shriek, followed with:

"Mercy me! Who has dared to leave a foundling on my step?"

And then, as she bent over and poked the pieces of blanket aside:

"Mercy! What a horridly homely brat!"

"It isn't!" exploded Hoof, in an undertone, as he snatched the handkerchief from his mouth. "Gracious! Wouldn't I like to pinch her!"

But Miss Lowthry must have recognized her duty as a citizen, for she picked up the basket and bore it into the house, slamming the door behind her.

"Wow! Oh, dear! oh, dear!" laughed a lot of mischievous youngsters hidden in the bushes.

"Look!" whispered Dave Darrin. "She has taken the basket into her sitting room. She's placed it on a table. There she goes to the telephone. Whee! See how she's working her arm, jerking that telephone bell crank!"

Some conversation that the young peepers, of course, couldn't hear passed over the telephone. Then Miss Lowthry hung up the receiver and thrust her forefingers into her ears as she turned to stare at the human contents of the basket on the table.

"The poor kid's hollering," muttered Hoof. "Can you blame it?"

All that followed, and which the boys could see through the lighted windows of the room interested them mightily. But at last they heard a heavy step on the sidewalk. Then one of the blue-coated guardians of Gridley's peace turned in at the gate, went up to the door and rang the bell.

"She sent for the police," chuckled Dick Prescott.

"Of course," grinned Dave.

The peeping boys saw the officer step through into the old maid's sitting room. Miss Lowthry pointed at the basket in a highly dramatic way. The policeman bent over to take a kindly look at the tiny youngster therein, then adjusting the pieces of blanket, he lifted the basket.

"Now, it's time to do your turn, Hoof," whispered Dick, giving young Sadby a nudge. "Slip over the fence and do it right."

Miss Lowthry followed the policeman to the door, opening it for him and letting him out.

"Boo-hoo!" sounded a heart-broken voice out on the sidewalk, in the darkness beyond. Then, as the policeman stepped down from the steps, Hoof suddenly let out a wail and darted into the yard.

"Say, Mister Cop, have you got it?" demanded Hoof eagerly.

"Got what?" demanded the policeman.

"My baby brother! You see, Mister Cop, some fellows took my baby brother and carried him off for a joke."

Then Hoof came into the pale light that was shed just past the open front door. There were tears in his eyes, all right, for an onion was one of the things that "Wrecker" Lane had brought from home. Hoof had rubbed a slice of the onion on the skin under his eyes, and the tears that he wanted to show were genuine enough.

"Is this your brother?" demanded the policeman, lowering the basket he was carrying.

The Sadby baby had begun to cry again, but at sight of Hoof the little fellow stopped suddenly, crowed and reached out with its little hands.

"After that do you have to ask if that's my kid brother?" demanded Hoof Sadby proudly.

"I guess it is, all right, Sadby," replied the policeman. "I know you. Well, if this is your brother, please take him off my hands—and welcome. You see, Miss Lowthry, it was nothing but the humorous prank of some boys. This is Hallowe'en."

"Boys!" sniffed Miss Lowthry, glaring. "Humph! I think I could eat a couple of boys, right now, if I could see them skinned alive and then boiled."

Hoof, once he had possession of the basket, raced away as though nothing else on earth mattered. This was good policy for, if he lingered, the policeman might begin to ask questions.

When the door had closed and the officer was gone, Dick and his crowd slipped out from concealment, joining Hoof and his baby brother.

"Oh, me, oh, my!" groaned Dave Darrin, stifling with laughter. "We must play this on some more folks."

"But say," warned Dick Prescott, "don't you think that, by the time we've played this on three or four more people, the policeman will begin to be suspicious of Hoof's wailing accents and his great joy at finding his kid brother?"

"Oh, we'll have to try it again, anyway," urged Tom Reade. "I know just the people to work it on. You know Mr. and Mrs Crossleigh? They live around on the next street. They haven't any children, and they're big cranks."

CHAPTER XVIII

CARRYING "FUN" TO THE DANGER LIMIT

The Hallowe'eners hidden across the street, and Hoof Sadby posted up the street, ready to come on the scene and do his part when needed, Tom Reade and Greg Holmes crept up to the front porch of the Crossleigh home, deposited the basket, rang and then bolted.

In a short time a dim light was visible through the stained glass of the front door. Then that barrier itself was opened, and Mr. Crossleigh, a man past middle age, and in dressing-gown and slippers, came out.

Seeing no one, and coming further out, Mr. Crossleigh almost kicked the basket. But he recovered in time, and bent down.

The peepers, not far away, heard him utter an exclamation of amazement. Then:

"Wife!" he called back into the house. "Come and see who's here!"

"Who is it?" hailed a voice from inside. "Cousin Jenny?"

"No; it isn't."

"Who? The minister?"

"No; you just come and see."

Then Mrs. Crossleigh came down the hallway and out on to the porch.

"Now, who do you think it is?" chuckled Mr. Crossleigh, lifting the basket.

"Henry Crossleigh, where on earth——"

"Don't ask me where it came from, wife. I found it here on the stoop when I answered the bell."

"Well of all the——" gasped the woman in wonder.

"Ain't it!" agreed her husband.

"It's—it's—why, I do believe it's a real cute little shaver," continued the woman hesitatingly.

"Fine little fellow, I should say, though I'm no judge," continued Mr. Crossleigh.

"And it isn't crying a bit. Do you suppose it's a foundling, left on our stoop, as we sometimes read of in the papers, Henry?"

"That's just what it is, of course. Folks don't leave small children around for a joke, wife."

"And have we got to take it in and keep it?"

"The law doesn't compel us to." "But—

Henry——"

"What is it, wife?"

"Do you suppose—we've never had any children. Do you think we could ——"

"We can do whatever you say, wife," nodded

"Is This the Brother You're Looking For?"

Mr. Crossleigh. "If you say that you want to——"

Here he came to a pause. The new idea was so wholly strange that he couldn't grasp it all at once.

Here Hoof Sadby, straining his ears from the distance, judged that it was high time for him to use his slice of onion. Then his doleful voice was heard as he came wailing along.

"Why, who's that out there?" cried Mrs. Crossleigh.

"Say, have you got my baby brother!" demanded Hoof, halting at the gateway, then running forward for a minute. "Some fellers——

"Is this the brother you're looking for?" asked Mr. Crossleigh, stepping toward Hoof, basket in hand.

"Yes!" snapped Hoof, giving a pretended gulp of joy. But, truth to tell, he felt so ashamed of himself that he was a poor actor at this moment. Had the Crossleighs been more suspicious they would have detected something sham in Hoof's beginning grief and his swift change to joy.

"Oh, thank you, sir," awkwardly sobbed Hoof, taking the basket. "I know the fellows that did this to me. They think this is a good Hallowe'en joke."

"I'm glad, boy, that you didn't have a longer hunt," remarked Mr. Crossleigh. "Good night!"

Then Hoof and the peepers across the way saw Mr. Crossleigh throw an arm around his wife's waist and draw her into the house, closing the door.

"Say, who said they were cranks?" demanded Greg Holmes, when the abashed Hallowe'eners had gathered a little way down the street. "Why, those folks would have been only too glad to take the little shaver in and——"

"Adopt it," supplied Dan Dalzell.

Truth to tell, Dick and all the Grammar School boys had seen the beginning of a scene that made their joke look small.

"If I ever catch any fellow trying to sneak the Crossleigh's gate," warned Dave loftily, "I'll give that fellow all that's coming his way!"

"They're the right sort of people," confessed Dick. "Fellows, we've all got to make it our business to see that the Crossleighs are never bothered again by fellows out for larks. Say, they showed us that playing a joke with a baby is only a clownish trick, didn't they?"

"I'm going home," announced Hoof. "This little shaver has been out long enough. It's time he was in his crib."

To this no objection was offered. As Wrecker Lane was near his home he ran off with the basket, which he tossed into the yard, after which he overtook his companions.

"What are we going to do, now?" Ben Alvord wanted to know.

"Let's prowl around and see what other Hallowe'eners are doing," proposed Dick.

Apparently there was enough going on. The Grammar School boys came across one party of grown young men who had climbed to the top of a blacksmith shop and had hoisted a wagon into place on the ridge pole. At another point they came across a group of High School boys who, with bricks done up in fancy paper, and with a confectioner's label pasted on the package, were industriously circulating these sham sweets by tying the packages to door-knobs, ringing the bells and then hurrying away. In another part of the town the Grammar School boys came upon a bevy of schoolgirls engaged in the ancient pastime of "hanging baskets."

In time Dick and the rest of the crowd found themselves down by the railroad, not far from the railway station. Lights shone out from the office where the night operator was handling train orders and other telegrams.

"What can we do here?" demanded Ben Alvord.

"I don't know," returned Dave.

"It's a bad place to play tricks," advised Dick. "Railway people are in a serious line of business, and they don't stand for much nonsense."

"Green is the night operator, and I don't forget the switching he gave some of us a year ago," muttered Ben Alvord bitterly.

"What were you doing?" asked Dick.

"Oh, just catching on and off a night freight that was being made up in the yard."

"And taking a big chance of getting hurt?" asked Dick. "I don't know that I blame Green much for taking the quickest course he knew of getting you out of harm's way."

"He had no right to switch us with a stick," insisted Ben.

"You're right he hadn't," spoke up another youngster. "I was there, and I got some of that switch across my legs, too. Whew! I can feel the sting yet."

"I guess it's about time that Green heard from us," insisted Ben.

"If I were you I wouldn't do anything around here," advised Dick.

"You're right," nodded Dave. "And I guess, Ben, you fellows didn't get a bit more than you deserved."

"I'll show old Green whether we did," snapped Ben.

"Don't you think of it," warned Greg Holmes. "It's a serious business to monkey with railroad property. Besides, anything serious might put in danger the lives of people traveling on the railroad."

"Oh, keep quiet and do some thinking," retorted young Alvord. "Any of you fellows that never eat anything but milk, and are 'fraidcats, can cut out of this. I tell you, I'm going to get hunk with Green, and fellows with sand, who want to see it, can stay. The milksops can go home and to bed."

Not a boy stirred away just then. It isn't boy nature to withdraw under taunts.

"Say, Ben, I'll tell you something you dassent do," dared one of the boys.

"It'll have to be something pretty big that I don't dare do," boasted young Alvord.

"Do you dast to pick up a stone and smash one of the red or green lights over there?"

The lights referred to were the signal lights for passing trains.

"Don't do that!" protested Dick Prescott sharply. "That certainly would be downright criminal!"

"Milksop!" retorted Ben. "I dast to do anything that I want to."

"I think I dare do anything that's decent," retorted Dick quietly. "But I don't pretend that I'm brave enough to commit crimes, if you call breaking the law bravery."

"Crime?" sneered Ben. "Bosh! This is only fun, and getting square with a man who has been mean to some of us."

"If you don't take Dick's advice, and cut out the trick, you'll be mighty sorry afterwards," urged Tom Reade. "Come on, fellows. Let's move along and find some fun that is more decent."

"Babies!" jeered Ben Alvord. "You haven't nerve enough to stand up for your rights and pay Green back for the way he treats the fellows when he loses his temper. You're babies! Go on. Those who aren't babies will stay right here and see what happens."

"You're talking boldly enough, now, Ben Alvord, but you'll be whining to-morrow, instead. Come on, fellows; let's have nothing to do with the scheme," cried Dick.

"Babies!" sneered Ben again. "You fellows who want to be classed with the babies can go. The fellows with nerve can stay right here."

"Come along, then," urged Dick, and he and his chums started away. At the corner, just before turning up the street that led away from the railway station Dick turned to see if others than his chums were coming along. But Dick & Co. proved to be the only ones who had left the scene.

There were others who wanted to go with Dick Prescott, but they didn't care to risk being taunted with being "babies." So they stood by Ben, though nervously.

"Do you s'pose we'll get in jail?" whispered one of Ben's followers nervously.

"Humph! You'd better run along with the babies," jeered Ben Alvord. "I guess it's time that some of you were in your cradles, anyway."

"Shut up! We're standing by you, aren't we?" Wrecker Lane demanded.

"Are you ready, then?" inquired Ben, glancing around at those who had stayed with him.

"Yes," replied Toby.

"Now, take good aim!" warned Ben, in a conspirator's tone. "Remember, we can't wait, this time, for any repeat shots. All you fellows ready?"

"Yes," came the response.

"When I say 'three,' then," ordered Ben. "All ready! One, two, three!"

Through the air whizzed a volley of stones.

Crash! Both the red and the green lights went out, the glass flying in splinters.

Guessing what had happened, Operator Green dashed out hotfoot in pursuit.

CHAPTER XIX

BEN WANTS TO KNOW WHO "BLABBED"

"Cheese it! Scoot!" sounded the unnecessary warning.

A crowd of boys, engaged in mischief, doesn't have to wait to be instructed in the art of vanishing.

By the time that Mr. Green, swift though he was, got out into the open, Ben and the other stone-throwers had scattered in as many different directions as there were boys in the party.

For a moment Night Operator Green halted, baffled, for every one of the fugitives had found safe cover.

"They've run down to the street, and are making off," decided the night operator, with bad judgment. "I'll catch some of them yet."

Whereupon he sprinted down to the corner and turned up the street. True enough he beheld a clump of boys, but they were gathered around one of their number and talking earnestly.

"Stop, you young heathen! Stay right where you are, if you know what's good for you!" yelled the angered operator.

None of the six boys moved more than was necessary in order for them to get a view of the charging operator.

"Now, I've got you;" roared Mr. Green swooping down upon Dick & Co.

"Well, Mr Green?" inquired Dick unafraid, as he had a right to be.

"I want all your names!" growled the operator. "Your right names, too!"

"I guess you know all of our names now, if you take a good look at us," smiled Prescott.

"Yes, I do," nodded Mr. Green grimly. "I wouldn't have thought it of any of you boys, either. But there's no telling what boys won't do nowadays."

"What are we supposed to have done?" Dick queried.

"You're the youngsters who threw a volley of stones and broke the railroad signal lights."

"Guess again!" suggested Dave.

"Aren't the lights broken, and didn't I catch you moving away from the scene?" glared Mr. Green.

"Yes; but didn't you hear some other boys getting away at the same time?" demanded Prescott.

"Um! I—er—suppose I did."

"Doesn't it strike you that the boys who broke your signal lights were the ones who ran away so fast?"

"Then you boys didn't do it!"

"We certainly didn't."

"Who were the boys, then!"

"Excuse me, Mr. Green, but you'll have to find that out for yourself."

"Who were they?" pressed the operator.

"As I said before, Mr. Green, you'll have to find that out for yourself."

"Then I guess I'll take you youngsters in on the charge. You know that I belong to the railway police, don't you?"

"Yes; and I also know," smiled Dick steadily, "that, if you don't succeed in proving your charge, you'll lay both yourself and the railroad liable to damages for false arrest."

Mr. Green looked a bit uneasy. This is a point of law intended to restrain officers of the law from making arrests without evidence.

"For the last time, will you tell me the names of the boys who threw the stones?"

"No," Dick rejoined, "for we don't know exactly what boys did the throwing."

"Name the boys you suspect, then."

"Nothing doing," Dave Darrin interposed, with emphasis.

"Then I'll have to take you boys in."

"That's your privilege—and your risk, as Dick has explained," laughed Dave.

Green fidgeted. He didn't want to make any mistakes, but he did wish that these Grammar School boys could be scared more easily.

"Will you come back to the station with me, without going in arrest?" asked the operator.

"Why?" questioned Prescott, pointedly.

"Because I'm going to send for the chief of police, and I shall want him to talk with you," Green answered.

"The chief of police knows where to find any of us when he wants to," hinted Darrin.

"If Mr. Green asks us to go to the railway station with him, without being placed under arrest, I don't see what harm that can do, fellows. What do you say if we accept Mr. Green's invitation?"

"All right," agreed some of the six. Even Dave consented.

Ten minutes later the chief of police was on hand. He inspected the broken lights just before the operator placed out new ones. Mr. Green stated what he knew of the affair. Then the chief turned to Dick & Co. He put many questions. Some of these Dick and his friends answered promptly. They even told how they had spoken against the proposed prank, and how they had left when they had found that the other boys couldn't be stopped. But as to the matter of naming the other boys all six refused.

"We're not tell-tales," Dick explained.

"Justice Lee can make you tell," warned the chief of police.

"Can he?" inquired Dick. "Can he make us testify as to our suspicions? And wouldn't warrants have to be issued for us before we could be taken to court?"

"No; the judge could issue summons for you all."

"But could he make us testify as to suspicions—things we didn't actually see?" propounded Dick Prescott.

The chief chewed the ends of his moustache.

"It's a criminal act to destroy the signal lights of a railway," the police officer went on. "You ought to tell us, to serve the ends of justice."

"Do you know what would happen to us?" Dick demanded.

"What?"

"Every other fellow in town would point his finger at us and cry 'tell-tale!' We'd get thrashed whenever we showed our heads outdoors."

"The police can protect you," declared the chief.

"Have you ever had policemen enough yet to prevent boys from fighting in Gridley?" challenged Dick, though his tone was respectful. "Besides, the thrashings wouldn't be anything to the scorn and contempt that we'd meet everywhere."

"You ought to tell us," insisted the chief of police. "You're helping to defeat the ends of justice."

"Aren't men clever enough to catch a few boy offenders, without demanding that other boys 'queer' themselves with every fellow in town?" insisted Dick.

"Justice Lee will make you tell, then," promised the chief, with a shake of his head.

"He can't!" spoke Dick with spirit. "I'll go to prison, and stay there, before I'll turn blab. So will my friends."

"That's just what we'll do," nodded Dave, his eyes flashing.

The chief chewed his moustache thoughtfully. At last he spoke.

"You boys can go now. I know where to find you when I want you."

Dick & Co. lost no time in getting away from this uncomfortable examination.

"Prescott and Darrin are regular little schoolboy lawyers, Green," laughed the chief. "We can't make them tell a thing."

"But the judge ought to be able to."

"Perhaps Justice Lee has the power, Green, but we'd only make heroes of Prescott, Darrin and the rest if we made martyrs of them in court. It would stir up a lot of bad feeling in the town, too, and after that every boy would feel that he had a grudge against you railway people. You'd be annoyed in loads of ways that the police couldn't very well stop. Prescott scored a hit with me when he said that a lot of grown men ought to be able to catch a lot of boy offenders. Green, the best thing to do is to put the case up to your railway company."

"The boys who threw the stones must be found and punished!" insisted the operator firmly.

"Yes; I agree with you on that point. But you'd better go about in a regular way. Wire your headquarters and ask that a railway detective be sent here on the case. My department will give your detective all proper aid in the matter."

One of the earliest trains, the next morning, brought Detective Briscoe. That official, however, worked very quietly. No one guessed who or what he was until he was ready to strike.

Ned Allen, Ben Alvord, Toby Ross, Wrecker Lane and Spoff Henderson were badly scared that same next morning. They met on the way to school and took blood-curdling oaths as to secrecy.

Then, in the school yard, Ben Alvord hunted up Prescott.

"Dick, you didn't give our names last night, did you?"

"No," Prescott replied.

"You won't name us, either, will you?"

"No, sirree!"

So the light-smashers felt more comfortable. By the day following they breathed easily—until they reached school.

The boys were in the yard, playing until the gong rang for morning session. A buggy drove up, and Detective Briscoe and two policemen in plain clothes got out.

"Trouble!" was the word whispered. Ben Alvord and his fellows turned pale. But the gong rang. Glad of any chance to bolt, Ben, Spoff, Ned, Toby and Wrecker fled to the basement to get into line.

Briscoe and the two policemen appeared in Old Dut's room. The detective drew some papers from his pocket, inquiring:

"You have boys here by the names of Allen, Alvord, Ross, Lane and Henderson, haven't you?"

"Yes," nodded Old Dut.

"Ask them to step forward, please."

Pallid and shaking a bit, the five came forward.

"Boys," announced Detective Briscoe, "I am sorry to say that Justice Lee wants to see you about a little matter on Hallowe'en. Get your hats and coats and come along."

An awed hush crept over the eighth grade room after the youngsters had left.

"I hope," declared Old Dut to his class, "that the young men haven't been doing anything very wrong."

Under Justice Lee's questioning the five broke down, one after another and confessed.

"Young men," said Justice Lee severely, "this is a more serious offense than probably any of you understand. Destroying railway signals is always likely to lead to destruction of property and even loss of life. I advise the parents of these young men to explain to them carefully and earnestly what a criminal thing these boys have done. If any of you young men are ever brought before me again, on such a charge, I shall send the offenders to a reformatory, there to remain until they are twenty-one. For this first offense I trust that the parents will act as my allies. On this occasion, therefore, I shall let the young men off with a fine of ten dollars each."

The fines were paid. Ben and his comrades reached school just as the afternoon session was closing. All five of the culprits were in an angry, defiant frame of mind.

"Whoop! There's Ben Alvord," shouted one of the eighth grade boys, as Central Grammar "let out." "Hullo, Ben! What did they do to you?"

"How long you got to go up for, Ben?" jeered another.

The five were quickly surrounded and eagerly questioned.

"That judge was too fresh!" declared Alvord wrathfully. "He called us criminals, and gave us a fierce scolding. He made our folks pay ten dollars apiece."

"That don't cost you anything," grinned one of the boys.

"Don't it, though?" Ben demanded angrily. "I had ten dollars and forty cents saved up for a bicycle. Dad said that, as long as I liked such expensive amusements, I could just pay the fine out of my bicycle money. So, now, I've got only forty cents left. And all because some fellows can't keep their mouths shut!"

"What do you mean by that, Ben?" demanded three or four fellows.

"I mean that Dick Prescott and his gang had to go and blab on us!" charged Ben Alvord. "There he is, now, the sneak!"

There was a great bobbing of heads. All eyes, and most of them accusing eyes, were turned on Dick & Co.

CHAPTER XX

DICK'S ACCUSER GETS TWO ANSWERS

Dick took a step forward, his face grave but his eyes steady as he faced his accuser.

"Ben, I know you're sore, but if you say that I, or any of my friends told on you, then you're going too far."

"You did!" asserted young Alvord. "You blabbed!"

"I didn't, and we didn't; not one of us."

"That's all right to say after you're caught," flared Ben.

"Then you call us liars?" flashed Dave Darrin, pushing his way forward, his fists clenched.

"You are, if you say you didn't blab!" panted Ben.

"Fight! fight!" chorused some of the boys.

"Get back, Dave, and keep cool," warned Dick, pushing his chum to the rear. "This thing started with me, and it's my affair first of all. Ben Alvord, look at me! I don't want to fight. I don't believe in fighting when it can be helped. I know you're sore, too, for you've just had a rough time of it after what you thought was fun on Hallowe'en. But you're going too far when you say we blabbed on you, for we didn't."

"Who did, then?" sneered Ben.

"I don't know. I'm not the chief of police. But, just because you can't think who told on you, you needn't come along and accuse us."

"I say you did tell—you or some of your gang!" retorted Ben.

"It sounds likely enough. No one else knew," muttered a boy on the outskirts of the crowd.

"Of course Dick Prescott or some of his gang told on us," insisted Ben Alvord angrily.

Dick took a step closer to his accuser.

"Then, Ben, you're a liar!" Prescott announced coolly.

"Punch him!" urged another boy, giving Ben a shove toward Dick.

"You bet I will!" snapped Alvord. "I don't allow a sneak to call me a liar."

"You can have a fight, if you insist on it," agreed Dick promptly. "You can have it right away, too, and it will last as long as you want. But this is no place. Let's go up to the field where we used to practise football."

"Whoop! Come on!" The crowd of Grammar School boys surged around the prospective fighters. A big procession started up the road.

"See here, this whole crowd can't come. So many will get us into trouble," shouted Dave.

"I'll name ten of Dick's friends, and Ben can name ten of his friends. No one else will be allowed to come."

Dave quickly called off his list of boys.

"Choose me, Ben!" "Choose me!" urged two score boys whom Dave had not named. Ben looked around, trying to select those whom he thought most friendly to himself.

Then the procession started again, containing only the chosen ones. Others wanted to go, but knew they would be driven back by the selected twenty friends.

The field was quickly reached. Ben Alvord was cooling, now. He would have drawn out of the fight, but knew that he couldn't get out without discredit. So Ben pulled off his jacket, took off his collar and tie and made ready.

Dick, who was almost wholly free from anger, made similar preparations. After a good deal of disputing Hoof Sadby was agreed upon as a referee satisfactory to both sides. Dave, of course, seconded Dick, while Alvord chose Toby Ross.

"Get your men forward," ordered Hoof. "Want to shake hands before you start?"

"No," growled Ben sullenly.

"Time, then! Get busy!"

Dick threw himself on guard. He was not an amazingly good boxer, but he had been through a few schoolboy fights.

"I'll knock your head off and wind it up!" blazed Ben, darting forward.

Instead of carrying out his programme, Ben received a blow on the nose that staggered him.

"No fair!" howled Ben, retreating. "I hadn't my guard up."

"Your fault, then," mocked Dick.

"All fair," chimed in Hoof. "Stop talking and mix it up."

Ben soon advanced once more, rather disconcerted by the wholly steady bearing of Dick Prescott.

This time Alvord tried to foul by hitting below the belt. Dick sidestepped and drove in a blow against Ben's left eye.

"My! That was a socker!" yelled some of the spectators.

"You're hitting too hard. It ain't fair," wailed Ben, backing off.

"If all you want is gymnastics you don't need me," mocked Dick. "Fight, if you're going to. If you're not, then get out of this."

"Mix it up!" ordered Hoof tersely, and the crowd took up the cry.

Ben suddenly let loose. For a few moments he kept young Prescott pretty busy. Not all of Ben's blows were fended off, either. Dick's face began to show red spots from the hard impacts of Alvord's tough little fists.

"Good boy, Ben! Go in and wind up his clock!" came the gleeful advice. "You've got him started. Keep him going!"

Just then a blow under the chin sent Ben down to the ground.

"Keep back, Prescott. Don't hit him while he's down," cried several. But this Dick had no intention of doing. Panting slightly, he waited for Ben to get to his feet. This Alvord soon did, drawing away crouchingly.

"Got enough?" hailed Dick.

"I'll show you!" raged Ben, rushing forward.

Dick met him half-way, in a leap. Now it was Prescott on the offensive, and he forced Ben all over the field, to the tune of encouraging yells. Ben tried to save his face, but couldn't. Then Dick hammered his body. Young Alvord lost all his coolness, and began to windmill his hands. That settled it, of course. Any boy who forsakes his guard to take to windmilling is as good as whipped. Dick watched his chance, then drove in a blow on Ben's jaw that felled him flat.

"O-o-oh!" wailed Ben, holding to his jaw with both hands.

"Do you give it up?" demanded Hoof.

"No!"

"Then get up and go on with the fight."

"I will when I'm ready."

"You will, now, or I'll decide against you," warned Hoof.

"That booby broke my jaw," groaned Ben.

"You wag it pretty well, for a broken jaw," jeered Dave.

"Get up, Ben!"

"If you don't you're thrashed!"

"Don't give up like a baby!"

"Get up and fight," ordered Hoof. "One!"

Ben lay on the ground, glaring about him in sullen silence.

"Going to get up?" demanded Hoof. "Two!"

"Oh, Ben, don't let Prescott whip you as easily as that," implored several of Alvord's backers.

"Get up!" commanded Hoof, putting the toe of his boot lightly against Alvord's body. "Three!"

Still Ben refused to stir.

"Dick Prescott wins the fight," announced Hoof judicially. "Ben refused three times to get up and go on."

As soon as Prescott began to don his discarded coat, Ben got to his feet.

"Now, I have something to say to you, Alvord," announced Dave, going over to the worsted one. "You insulted six of us and called us liars. Dick is only one. You'll have to fight the rest of us, one a day, or else apologize before the crowd."

"I won't apologize," glared Ben.

"All right, then. You'll fight me after school to-morrow," Darrin declared.

"And me the day after," challenged Greg Holmes. Reade, Dalzell and Hazelton all put in their claims for dates.

"You think you're going to bully me, don't you?" grunted Ben.

"No," Dave answered. "But when a fellow lies about me I'm going to make him fight or apologize."

"I don't know whether I will fight you, or not," snarled Ben.

"Then you'll get a thrashing just the same, and be called a coward by every decent fellow in school," flared Dave.

Ben quailed a bit inwardly. He had had all the fighting he wanted for the present.

"That Prescott fellow is no good, anyway," sniffed Ben, as he walked homeward with Toby Ross, the only one of the late spectators who had stood by him.

"Well, may-be he didn't tell on us," suggested Toby.

"'Course he did!"

"Dick has always acted pretty decently."

"Huh! If neither he nor any of his gang told, then who did?" demanded Ben, as though that settled it.

"Ben Alvord, what have you been doing?" demanded his mother, as Ben showed up at the kitchen door.

"Why?"

"Your face is all bruised. Have you been fighting?"

"Yes, ma'am. I had to. I thumped Dick Prescott for telling on us and getting us all arrested."

"Did Dick say that he told on you?" asked Mrs. Alvord.

"No, ma'am."

"Denied it, didn't he?"

"Yes'm."

"And I guess Dick told the truth. I know who did tell on all you boys," announced his mother.

"Who?" demanded Ben sullenly.

"Your little brother, Will."

Willie Alvord was only between four and five; not yet old enough to go to school.

"I got it all out of the baby this afternoon," continued Mrs. Alvord. "I saw him playing with a new baseball bat, and I made him tell me where he got it. It seems that Willie heard you and Toby, and the other boys talking about your Hallowe'en pranks yesterday morning before you went to school. Then, later, Willie was out in the street playing, when 'a nice man'—as Willie called him—came along and got to talking with him. The man talked about you, it seems, Ben, and he made believe he didn't think Willie's big brother was very smart. Then Willie up and boasted of your smartness down at the railroad.

The 'nice man' took Willie to the corner and bought him some candy and a baseball bat, and kept on talking about you and Toby, and the rest, and of course Willie told the 'nice man' all he'd heard about the railroad business."

"That 'nice man' must have been the detective," growled Ben. "Oh, he's a real 'nice man.' If Willie was larger I'd take the baseball bat to him for talking too much!"

"Well, you won't," warned his mother dryly. "Willie is only a baby, and didn't know what he was saying. But you'd better go and apologize to Dick Prescott."

"Huh!" was Ben's undutiful retort. Then he went outside with Toby.

"So Dick didn't tell?" mused Toby. "It was your kid brother?"

"Don't you tell that to any one!" warned Ben Alvord,flushing.

"Why, you'll have to tell it yourself," protested Toby. "You'll surely have to beg Dick Prescott's pardon after what you said to him before the whole crowd. If you don't, then I'll tell myself. I'm not going to see Dick blamed for what he didn't do."

"If you blab to any one," warned Ben angrily, "I'll give you a good thrashing."

"Try it, and perhaps you'll get more of what Dick gave you this afternoon," Toby shot back as he walked through the gate.

Toby was as good as his word. He told the news at school the next day, and Ben Alvord's stock went even lower. After school that afternoon Dave Darrin made Ben apologize. So did Reade, Holmes, Hazelton and Dalzell. It was a bitter pill for young Alvord to swallow. The fights that the other chums had claimed were now called off. They felt Ben to be beneath their notice.

CHAPTER XXI

AB. DEXTER MAKES A NEW MOVE

"Did you hear the latest from Ab. Dexter?" asked Dave, as he met Dick one Saturday afternoon in November.

"No; nothing very good, was it?"

"That's hardly to be expected," laughed Dave, as the two chums came to a halt on a street corner. "Did you happen to remember that Dexter and Driggs were due to come up for trial in court this afternoon?"

"No; I had forgotten the date."

"Well, this was the day. Justice Lee, if you remember, bound them over to answer at court."

"Yes; I remember that."

"Well, neither of them showed up, and so the court declared forfeited the cash bail that Dexter put up for the pair."

"The money ought to be worth more to the county than both men put together," laughed Dick.

"I guess that's the way the court looked at it."

"I hope Dexter and Driggs are both a mighty long way from Gridley, and that they will stay. Mrs. Dexter isn't having any bother at all, these days, is she?"

"You ought to be the one to know that," teased Dave. "You're the one she sends for whenever she takes it into her head that she wants to reward us for some jolly good fun that we had in helping her."

"I had a note from Mrs. Dexter a few days ago," Dick went on. "Maybe I forgot to tell you about it. She wanted me to call on her, and I wrote back that I was awfully sorry but that my evenings just then had to be put in getting ready for the monthly exams. I haven't heard a word from her since then."

"She's a fine woman," nodded Dave, "but she certainly has the reward habit in bad shape."

"Feels some like snow, doesn't it?" inquired Dick, looking up at a lead-colored sky.

"It'll rain," predicted Dave. "It isn't yet cold enough for snow."

"I'll be mighty glad when the snow comes."

"Maybe I won't," uttered Darrin. "That's the best time of the year—winter."

"Unless you call summer the finest time."

"Of course in summer we have the long vacation and plenty of time to have fun."

"Better duck," advised Dick suddenly. "Here comes Mrs. Dexter now."

"Looks as though she'd been crying, too," murmured Dave, scanning the approaching woman.

"Then we won't scoot," advised Dick, changing front instantly. "It doesn't look very fine to run away from any one who's in trouble."

Strangely enough Mrs. Dexter didn't appear, at first, to want to talk with the boys. She nodded, smiled wanly and said:

"Good afternoon, boys! Are things dull to-day?"

"Just quiet, Mrs. Dexter," Dick answered.

Then Dave, with some of his usual impulsiveness, put in, earnestly:

"You look as though you had heard bad news, Mrs. Dexter."

The woman had started to go on her way. Then she turned about again.

"Perhaps I have heard bad news," she smiled wearily.

"It isn't anything that we could help you about, is it?" asked Dick. He felt that he was taking a liberty in putting the question, yet he could not hold his inquiry back.

"I—I am afraid not, this time," she answered slowly. "Besides, I don't want to see any of you get into any more trouble on my account."

"Then it's—it's Mr. Dexter?" hazarded Dave.

The woman swallowed hard, seemed to be trying to choke back something, and then replied:

"Yes."

"Has he dared to get troublesome again?" flashed Dick.

"N-n-n-o matter. Please don't ask me. You can't help me any this time."

Once more Mrs. Dexter looked as though she would follow her way, but some other instinct prompted her to add:

"Don't think I don't appreciate my excellent young friends. But you can't help me this time. No one can. Mr. Dexter is too dangerous a man, and when he threatens disaster, and says he'll wait patiently a year to bring it about, he means every word that he says."

"Whew! So he has threatened that, has he?" Dick inquired.

"Yes. I guess I may as well tell you the rest of it. Well, this morning I received a letter from Mr. Dexter. He wanted more money before. Now he puts his demand at thirty thousand dollars. He says that, if I don't arrange to meet him and turn over the cash, he'll wait patiently for a year or more, if necessary, but that he'll watch and find his chance to burn my home down and destroy Myra and me in it."

"Dexter threatened that, did he?" chuckled Dave Darrin, almost merrily. "Why Dexter hasn't the nerve to do such a thing. Excuse me, Mrs. Dexter, but all that fellow is good for is frightening timid women."

"I wish I could believe that," sighed the woman nervously.

"You have a special policeman still in the house, haven't you, Mrs. Dexter?"

"Yes. He's there, now, watching over Myra."

"Well, at the worst," pursued Dick, "hire a second man and put him on guard nights outside the house, and you'll never hear from Dexter—except by mail, anyway. But how does the man expect you to send him word about the money? Did he give you any address?"

"He told me to put an advertisement, worded in a certain way, in the morning 'Blade.'"

"And—pardon me—you've been up and inserted the advertisement?" questioned Dick.

"Ye-es."

"And have arranged to get the money?"

"Yes; I've seen Mr. Dodge at the bank."

"When are you to meet Dexter!"

"When he sees my advertisement in the 'Blade' to-morrow he'll send me word where to meet him."

"You ought to send a detective, instead," blazed Dave Darrin.

"If I did, Dexter would wait his time and then destroy my child and myself," answered the woman, her under-lip quivering.

"You don't really believe that, do you?" asked Dave.

"No; I know it."

"You haven't been to see a lawyer, have you?" inquired Prescott.

"No; I don't dare that, for a lawyer would advise, as you did, sending a detective to keep the appointment, and then Mr. Dexter would be put in prison. I don't want Myra to grow up with the shame of having a father in prison. I—I am glad that Dexter jumped his bail on the other little charge."

"I see just this much about it, Mrs. Dexter," followed Dick. "But—you don't mind my speaking, do you?"

"No; I like to hear you, for you boys have already saved me some heartaches."

"What I was going to say, Mrs. Dexter, is that, no matter how much money you give that man, he'll always keep bothering you as long as you have any left. A man who won't work can't be very brave, and a man who doesn't work can spend an awful lot of money. If you surrender to Dexter I'm sure you'll have to keep on giving in just as long as you have any money left."

"Then you think I ought not to give him the money, and that I ought to hire another good man to guard the house outside?"

"Yes; if you 're really afraid. It'll be cheaper to hire another man than to give all your fortune away."

"But I've put the advertisement in the 'Blade.'"

"There's time enough to take it out."

"I—I believe I'll do that," murmured Mrs. Dexter. Talking with the boys had given her a new little rise in courage.

"That's what I'd do if it were my case," added Darrin.

"Thank you! I'll go right up and take the advertisement out at once."

As though afraid that her courage might fail her, if she delayed, Mrs. Dexter turned and walked rapidly back in the direction whence she had just come.

"There flies a pot of money out of Dexter's window!" grinned Dave.

"I'm far from being sorry," returned Prescott.

Though neither boy had paid any heed to the fact a cab had moved slowly down Main Street past them while Mrs. Dexter was talking. The curtains were drawn just enough to make the interior of the vehicle a black shadow. Lolling on the back seat, with one curtain adjusted just so that he could look out sufficiently, sat a man, disguised somewhat, though none the less Abner Dexter.

"My wife has been up to the 'Blade' office and has put an advertisement in," muttered Dexter. "Now, she's talking to those two meddlesome boys. About me, I wonder? Blazes! There she is, turning about again. I wonder if she's going back to take that advertisement out?"

The cab turned a corner. Then, on directions from inside, the driver moved his horses along at a brisk trot. The same cab was passing near the "Blade" office when Mrs. Dexter went there for a second time.

The next morning Ab. Dexter and Driggs unfolded a copy of the "Blade" between them.

"I've got a misgiving that we won't find the advertisement," muttered Dexter gloomily. "No, sir. It isn't here, Driggs. Hang the woman, and twenty times hang those meddling youngsters! Driggs, I never shall win while those confounded boys are loose in Gridley!"

"We'll take real care of 'em this time," muttered Driggs, with an oath.

"We will!" confirmed Dexter. "We'll stop their troubling us!"

CHAPTER XXII

TRICKED INTO BAD COMPANY

The heads of fifty eighth grade pupils were bent over as many broad volumes on geography. It was study period; recitation would be called in five minutes.

Old Dut looked up from a report blank over which he had been poring, to shoot out this question:

"Why doesn't the tide rise and fall in inland rivers?"

It was a habit of Old Dut's to throw out questions like this in study time, for the purpose of waking up some of the intellects that needed rousing.

"Master Holmes, you may answer that," proclaimed the principal.

Greg started out of a brown study at hearing his name spoken. He had a vague recollection of having heard a question asked. But his mind was still far away, so he did not realize the enormity of his offense as he replied:

"I don't know, but I'll be the goat. What's the answer?"

A gasp of amazement sounded around the room.

"Master Gregory Holmes," uttered Old Dut sternly, "ten checks for that impertinence. And go and stand in the corner by the piano. Turn your back to the school that you've insulted!"

At that moment there came a rap on the door. Then a young man entered, handing a sealed envelope to the principal.

"Master Prescott, put your books away and come here," directed Old Dut.

The class looked on wonderingly, while Dick obeyed.

"Here is a note from your mother, which requests that you be allowed to go home at once, as your father has been injured in an accident. I hope, my boy, that it is nothing serious," said the principal in a low tone. "Your mother has sent a carriage in order that you may get home sooner. Go at once, Master Prescott, and may you learn that the news is not too bad."

Old Dut held out the note, but Dick barely saw it. Instead, he turned and ran to the coat room, caught up his coat and cap and sped downstairs. The messenger had already started downstairs.

"There's the rig," announced the messenger, as Dick appeared on the steps.

Alongside a surrey was drawn up. A rain curtain and side panels covered the rear seat, but the driver, a silent individual, who had a full, heavy red beard and wore smoked glasses over his eyes moved to make room for Dick on the front seat.

"How badly is dad hurt?" demanded Dick breathlessly, as he bundled himself in on the front seat.

"Can't say," replied the driver, in a low, weak voice. "I was only hired to come after you."

"Hurry!" appealed Dick. The driver nodded, and started the horse away briskly.

Young Prescott was fearfully worried. His mother was a woman of cool, calm judgment. She was not likely to send a driver after him unless his father's injuries were dangerous.

"I hope dad isn't going to die," breathed the boy to himself. "If he must, then I hope I get home in time before he goes."

So absorbed was he in his own gloomy thoughts that Dick gave no heed to the road that was taken. Nor had the surrey gone far when the rain curtain behind parted, but Prescott did not see that.

Yet he had no suspicion of foul play until a pair of hands from behind gripped him about the throat.

In a twinkling Dick was drawn over the back of the front seat. Then he vanished behind the curtain.

"Anybody in the street see that done, Driggs?" whispered the voice of Abner Dexter.

"Nary one," retorted Driggs, in a more natural voice than he had used before.

Though Dick Prescott was half strangled he heard both voices, now, and they sounded wholly natural to him. Driggs was disguised, but Dexter had taken no such pains.

"Now, you keep mighty quiet, or you'll be worse off than you thought your father was," snarled Ab. Dexter. He had Dick jammed down on the floor, the boy's head just above the man's lap. Dexter's fingers kept their fearful grip at the boy's throat.

Not that Dick didn't fight back. He fought with all his strength. Yet that was not for long. Dexter had taken a foul hold and had the boy at his mercy. The gripping at the throat continued until Dick's muscles relaxed and he was still.

"He'll come back to his senses, though, in a minute," uttered Dexter to himself. He drew out a big handkerchief and a bottle. There was an odor of something sickishly sweet in the air for a moment, as the handkerchief was pressed to the boy's nostrils.

All the time Driggs had continued to drive onward at a brisk trot.

"I've got to open up this curtain a bit, Driggs," called Ab. Dexter, in a not-too-loud voice. "I don't want to whiff in much of the stuff that I'm giving the youngster."

Yet, though some air was admitted to the rear part of the surrey Dexter took pains not to expose himself to the possibly too-curious glance of any passer on the street. At the same time the man bent over Dick, to note any signs of returning consciousness.

At last, seeing that second inhalation of the drug had rendered Dick wholly senseless, Dexter drew another handkerchief from a pocket, and with this he gagged the boy. Then, a moment later, he reached down and tied the youngster's hands.

It was in a direction very different from that of Dick's home that the surly, silent Driggs was driving. Before long he was out in the suburbs of the town, traveling up the back country into the hills.

"The cub will learn, this time," mused Dexter savagely. "If he doesn't, it will be because he's too stubborn to learn anything. And, in that case——"

After the first half hour the road grew wilder. After going some two miles up into the hills Driggs turned off at the right, following a road used only in winter, and then principally by wood-cutters. Thus on, farther and farther into the woods, and turning, now and then, off into branching roads.

Though given an occasional whiff of the stuff from the bottle, that kept him senseless, Dick was allowed to regain his wits after the surrey had branched off over the forest roads.

"Keep quiet and be a good boy," admonished Dexter grimly. "You don't want any more of the stuff, do you? Too much of it might wind you up for good. We don't want to go that far—if you've got sense enough to be of use to us at last."

"Where on earth are they taking me—and what for?" wondered Dick, struggling against the nausea that the inhaling of the drug had caused. "What's Dexter's newest piece of villainy, I wonder? Whew! But that was a slick trick! Anyway, dad can't be hurt at all. Mother would never pick them as the messengers to send for me! I'm glad dad's all right, anyway, even if I may happen to have a rough time ahead of me."

The messenger who had entered the schoolroom, it may be said in passing, was not in the plot, nor had he been aware that there was any one at all in the rear part of the surrey. That messenger had been picked up on the street, by Driggs, and had been offered a quarter to take the note upstairs to the principal's class room, "because," Driggs had explained, "I don't dare leave my horse."

"How on earth did this rascally pair ever manage to write a note that would look enough like mother's handwriting!" was Dick's next puzzle.

As this, of course, was beyond his fathoming, Dick's next and very natural thought was:

"What on earth do these scoundrels want of me? I don't believe they have brought me away just for vengeance."

"A nice ride like this, off amid the beauties of nature, is a whole lot better than spending your time over dull school books, isn't it?" Dexter asked mockingly.

But Dick could gain no idea as to the kind of country through which he was passing, more than that the surrey was moving over rough road. Jammed down where he was he could see nothing but the half dark interior of the vehicle.

At last Driggs began to whistle softly. That being a signal, Ab. Dexter again produced the bottle. There was the same sickening odor as a wet handkerchief was placed against Dick's nostrils. Then he lost track of what was happening.

"Whoa!" called Driggs and willingly enough the horse stopped. There was a ripping aside of the rubber side panels to the carriage, after which Driggs stood on the ground to receive the senseless boy as Dexter passed him out.

"Into the house, I suppose?" inquired Driggs.

"Yes," nodded Dexter.

"Go ahead, then, with the key, and open up."

The house stood at some distance from the road, and, in summer time, would have been hidden from the road. The house had not been occupied in a quarter of a century by any lawful tenant. It was a two story affair, and had been originally built for the superintendent of a lumber and milling camp. Beyond was a brook that had been dammed, furnishing good water-power for all the year excepting in the summer months. By the old water course lay the ruins of what had once been a saw-mill.

Running up the short flight of steps to the front door of the dilapidated old dwelling off in the forests, Ab. Dexter produced a rusty iron key and swung the door open.

"Where you going to put him?" asked Driggs.

"In the rear apartments, upstairs," answered Dexter, with a laugh.

Accordingly Dick was carried upstairs and into a roomy back apartment. There were inside shutters that Dexter swung open while Driggs dropped the breathing though unconscious Grammar School boy on the floor.

"Now, you'd better get that borrowed rig back in the part of the world where it belongs," advised Ab. Dexter.

"I will," nodded Driggs. "But—say!"

"Well?"

"That Prescott boy is young, but he's tricky."

"I know that, don't I?"

"Then, when he comes to, you won't let him play any trick on you that will give him a chance to bolt from here?"

"Not I," promised Dexter. "You needn't worry. There are too many thousands of dollars at stake. Run along, Driggs. I'll do my part, here on the scene."

Driggs went out. He had a long drive ahead of him. The point at which he intended to abandon the stolen surrey was nearly ten miles from the present spot. For the horse and surrey had been stolen from a farmer known to be away for the day with his family. Driggs meant to abandon the rig two or three miles from the farmer's home, and then return on a bicycle which he had hidden near the spot.

As soon as Driggs had gone, Dexter bent over, tying Prescott's hands more securely.

Soon after that Dick, still lying on the floor, opened his eyes.

CHAPTER XXIII

DICK MAKES HIS STAND FOR HONOR

Ab. Dexter's harsh voice jarred on the air.

"Welcome to our city, Prescott," he laughed.

Dick's first discovery was that the gag was gone from his mouth. He made an effort to use his hands, but discovered that these were more securely tied than ever.

"I hope you'll enjoy this little visit with us," laughed Dexter, changing his voice, which now sounded almost pleasant.

"I'd enjoy it a lot more," retorted Dick dryly, "if I had my chums here with me."

"I, too, wish we had them here," nodded Dexter. "But they'd be tied up, just as you are. You don't seem a bit curious as to why you're here."

"No," Dick admitted.

"Marvelous youth, in whom the instinct of curiosity is dead!"

"Whatever your game in bringing me here, I can guess that it's one that wouldn't interest honest men."

"Oh, you're going to turn 'fresh,' are you?"

Dick did not reply. Dexter drew a cigar out from a vest pocket, as he stood leaning against a decaying mantel, and lighted it. This imitation of a man smoked in silence for a few moments, during which Prescott did not offer to speak.

Going over to the table, and drawing a newspaper from one of his pockets, Dexter sat down to read. He did not take off his coat, for the room was chilly.

Dick did not move, nor did he offer to speak. In his present bad plight he would have been glad enough to talk with anything living, even with so despicable a human object as Ab. Dexter.

"But he'd only torment me, and try to scare me, too, probably," thought Dick. "I won't give him any chance that I can help."

It was wholly natural that the boy's obstinate silence, which endured for the next hour, should anger the man.

At last, after having consumed two cigars and read a lot of stuff in the paper in which he was not interested, Dexter rose and stepped over to the boy.

"Having pleasant thoughts, eh?" he demanded.

"Better than yours, I'm sure," retorted the boy dryly.

"Yes?"

"Yes; because my thoughts, at least, are clean and honest ones."

"Oh, you little saint!" jeered Ab.

"I'm hardly a saint, and am not sure that I'd care to be one. But at least I'm happier and better off than a bigger fellow who'd be a big scoundrel if he weren't too big a coward!"

"You mean that for me, do you?" snarled Dexter.

"You may have it if you like it!"

"You insolent little puppy!" snapped Ab., giving emphasis to his wrath by kicking him.

"I see that I was wrong," said Prescott quietly. "I intimated that you are a coward. I apologize. Only a brave man would kick a helpless boy."

The quiet irony of the speech made even Ab. Dexter flush.

"Well, I wasn't kicking a boy. I was kicking his freshness," explained Dexter, in a harsh voice. "And I'll kick a lot more of that freshness, if I have to."

"I don't doubt it. Women and boys are your choice for fighting material. And, if I had some of my chums here, you'd find kicking boys too perilous a sport."

"You won't have them here," laughed Ab. coarsely. "You're the only one of the six that I want, so the others can stay in Gridley."

"But they won't," declared Dick. "At least, not long, after they discover that I'm missing."

"They'll never discover you, unless you go back to town by my permission," jeered Dexter. "Here, I'll show you something."

Bending over, he seized the boy by his coat collar, next lifting and dragging Dick to a window at the rear.

"Look out, and tell me what you see," commanded the jailer.

"I see the woods, and a few other things," Dick replied. "And—yes, I know where I am. This is the house at Bannerman's old mill. I was up this way last year after nuts."

"You know, then, that you're a good way from where folks would look for you."

"Oh, I'm not so sure of that, Dexter. Dave Darrin and the rest of the fellows know all of this country. We've all tramped through here before. They're very likely to think of this place within the next day or two."

"If they don't get here before dark, and if you haven't done, by that time, what I brought you here to do, then they won't find you."

"No?" challenged Dick Prescott.

"Look again, and tell me what you see outside. Do you see that place where Driggs has been digging? Do you see the hole he started, and the shovel beside it? Can you guess how we could dig that hole deeper, and put something away in it?"

There was a derisive smile on young Prescott's face as he started to look. Then his expression changed. He did not start, cry out nor turn pale, but that smile vanished.

"You see it, don't you?" demanded Ab. Dexter, watching the boy's face.

"You want to scare me about that hole, I suppose?"

"Yes; if you haven't gotten around completely to my way of thinking before dark to-night Driggs may have to finish his digging."

"Does he need exercise?"

"You've guessed what I mean," declared Dexter, "although you pretend to misunderstand me."

"Humph!"

"Look out, Prescott, that you don't put us in an ugly temper."

But Dick had found his courage by this time. He laughed merrily, though it was forced.

"What are you laughing at?" asked the other.

"At the very idea, Dexter, of your having nerve enough to do a thing like that! Why, there are boys in the primary school in Gridley who have more real sand than you have."

For answer the scoundrel seized the boy, hurling him across the room. Dick tottered. Being unable to use his hands to aid himself, he fell to the floor and lay there.

"Do you know what you ought to be doing, Dexter?" inquired Dick, as soon as he had smothered his wrath a bit.

"Well?"

"You ought to be training puppies for the dog circus. Not by fear, you know, for you really couldn't scare anything. But, in training puppies by the golden rule you'd be at your best!"

"I'll train you before I get through with you," snarled the rascal.

"There's only one thing you need to make you rather funny," remarked Dick.

"What is that?"

"All you need to make you funny, Dexter, is a little more wit."

Ab. stepped over and administered another kick.

"Thank you," acknowledged Prescott politely.

"Much obliged, are you?"

"Yes; a kick from you is an honor. Only a handshake or a compliment would hurt."

Dexter's face showed his wrath. He would have retorted, but he felt his helplessness in a battle of wits alone against Dick Prescott.

For a moment or two Ab. left the room. Dick began immediately to test the security of the cords at his wrists. He found himself only too well tied. Dick glanced searchingly about, intent on finding something that promised help or escape.

But Ab. came back, carrying an oil heater and a book. Placing the lighted heater beside the table Dexter sat down and opened the book.

"I knew you had cold feet," laughed Dick. "I've been waiting for you to seek some way of warming up."

Ab. scowled, but went on reading his book. This time the silence was an extremely long one. It was not broken, in fact, until Dick had lost all track of time, and knew only that there was still some daylight left. At last a whistle sounded outside.

Dropping the book, Dexter made his way out into the hall, and thence downstairs. Again Dick began to tug at the cords around his wrists. Then Dexter came into the room, followed by Driggs.

“Well,” asked Driggs, “has the young cub come to his senses yet?”

“I haven’t tried him,” responded Ab. sourly. “You can take him in hand if you want, Driggs.”

“You hain’t told him what we want?”

“Not a word,” Ab. answered. “You can take him in hand. Don’t stand any nonsense, either.”

“It ain’t exactly my way to stand nonsense,” growled Driggs, who was a good deal more courageous than Dexter. “As a first step I’ll untie his hands. The boy can’t make any fight against the two of us.”

Instead of untying, however, Driggs opened his clasp knife, and cut the cords at Dick’s wrists, after which he untied the big handkerchief that had also been tied there.

"Now, get on your feet, Prescott."

Dick obeyed, taking his time about it. No matter what was about to happen Dick knew that he could take better care of himself standing up.

"Exercise your hands and arms a bit, if you want to," continued Driggs. "You may find that circulation has been stopped."

This Dick knew well enough. As his hands might be of extreme use to him in the very near future he followed the last bit of advice.

"Go get your writing materials," said Driggs, turning to Ab.

Dexter left the room, soon returning with paper, envelopes and a pen thrust down into a bottle of ink.

"Now, I'll tell you what you've got to do, boy," Driggs continued. "Or maybe you can tell him that better, Dexter."

"You're going to write a letter to Mrs. Dexter," stated Ab. "In that letter you're going to tell her that you're hopelessly in my power, and that you realize how foolish it is for her to refuse my demands any longer. So you're to advise her that the best thing for her—and the only hope of saving your life as well as hers—is for her to pay me that forty thousand dollars——"

"You've gone up ten in your price, haven't you?" asked Dick with a momentary lack of caution.

"So-ho!" muttered Ab. "Mrs. Dexter did tell you about my last letter when you were talking on Main Street last Saturday. And I suppose you advised her to go back to the 'Blade' office and withdraw the advertisement that my letter had frightened her into paying for."

Dick bit his lips in silence.

"Did you advise her that way, or didn't you?" insisted Ab. angrily.

"Whatever she and I may have said to each other is not going to be repeated here," Prescott answered.

"Oh, it isn't Mr. High-and-mighty?" sneered Driggs, going closer to the boy and laying a hard hand on him. "See here, youngster, you may have an idea that Dexter isn't very dangerous. You'll have a different notion about me, if I turn myself loose on you. Now, you get suddenly respectful. Answer straight, and do just what we tell you—or I'll take you in hand."

"I won't write any such letter as you order me to," retorted Dick stubbornly.

"You won't? I tell you you will!" roared Driggs, gripping Prescott by the collar. "Sit down at that table."

"I won't!"

"You will!"

Driggs lifted Dick fairly off his feet, shaking him roughly. A thirteen-year-old boy didn't have much chance against a brute of Driggs's strength. The latter slammed the boy into a seat at the table.

"Now, pick up that pen!"

Dick picked it up, but aimed it at the wall opposite, hurling it forcibly.

With an oath Ab. Dexter went over and picked up the pen.

"He's broken the nibs," growled Ab., coming back with the pen. "No matter, I have a pencil. If he breaks the point of that it can be sharpened again. Here's the pencil."

"Now, pick up that pencil," commanded Driggs hoarsely, "and write just what Dexter tells you to write. When you've written it you'll sign it. Then Dexter will enclose it with a letter from himself in which he'll tell Mrs. Dexter just where to meet him and pay over the money. If it ain't paid over, then slam you go into the hole that I've dug for you out back of here, and the dirt will go falling in on your face. Now—write!"

However slight a notion Dick might have concerning Dexter's nerve, he did not doubt that Driggs was really "bad." Here was a brute who might very likely carry out his threats. Yet Dick, in addition to possessing an amazing lot of grit for a boy of his age, had also a great amount of stubbornness about doing the right thing and not doing a wicked one.

"I don't know what you'll do to me, Driggs," the boy retorted, "and probably I can't hinder you any. But if you think I'm going to obey nasty loafers like you two, then you've made a poor guess."

"What's that?" roared Driggs. "I'll teach you!"

He caught Dick Prescott up with both hands, shaking the boy until it seemed as though all the breath had left the youngster's body. Next, Driggs held his victim with one hand while with the other he struck blows that all but rendered the Grammar School boy unconscious.

"Here, don't kill the boy just yet, Driggs," ordered Dexter.

"You mind your own business, now, Ab.," retorted Driggs, his face purple with passion. "Your milk-and-water way doesn't do any good. I'm in charge, now, and I'm sole boss as to what shall be done to this baby if he doesn't take our orders!"

Again Dick received a severe mauling. He tried to fight back, but Driggs held him off at arm's length. At last Driggs lifted the boy once more by his coat collar.

"Now, I'll finish you!" roared the brute. "That is, unless you holler out, mighty quick, that you're ready to write all that we tell you to write."

"That won't happen this year!" Dick flashed back recklessly.

"Oh, it won't, eh? Then so much the worse for you. I won't waste another second's time in coaxing you. Do you want to change your mind before I start?"

"No!" the Grammar School boy retorted doggedly.

CHAPTER XXIV

CONCLUSION

At heart young Prescott was frightened enough. Yet he was also aroused to a fury of resistance.

With an ugly growl Driggs started in to shake the lad once more. Just at this moment, however, Dick found a chance on which he had been doing some frenzied calculating.

As he hung from Driggs's outstretched hand Dick's foot was just about on a level with one of the fellow's knees. Dick drew his foot back like a flash, delivering a lusty kick.

The blow glanced. Even at that Driggs's knee-cap suffered. With a groan of pain Driggs let go and stood by to rub his injured knee.

"You young fiend!" hissed Ab. Dexter, grabbing Dick by the collar.

Driggs tried two or three limping steps.

"Anything broken there?" demanded Ab. anxiously.

"No; but I've got to have cold water to bandage it with, right away," replied Driggs. "Give me hold of the young pest's collar, and I'll hold him all right until you get in again. But hustle with the water."

By this time Driggs had sunk into one of the chairs. Ab. dragged the boy to him and the other ruffian took vindictive hold.

"I'll settle with you, you little varmint, after I get my knee attended to," growled Driggs. "If you try any more tricks I'll let even my knee go and choke the life out of you."

Dick Caught Up the Other Chair.

Dexter hurried from the room. Dick, who felt that seconds must be made to count now, turned like a flash, sinking his teeth in the wrist of the hand that gripped his collar.

"You young——" began Driggs, in a wild temper, starting to rise from the chair as the pain forced him to let go of Dick's collar.

But Prescott, moving only two steps, caught up the other chair, bringing it down on the head of the ugly rascal.

"Dexter! Dexter—quick!" roared Driggs. "The boy's getting away!"

It was dark now, in the lower hall, as Dick, darting down the stairs, made out the form of Ab. Dexter as the latter hastened in through the outer door.

"Out of the way, or I'll hurt you with Driggs's knife!" panted the fleeing boy.

In that instant Abner Dexter proved Dick's suspicion that he was at bottom a coward. Ab. drew up close to the wall, and Dick, with the speed of the hunted deer, dashed from the house.

"It may take Ab. a little while to find that I haven't got Driggs's knife," grinned the boy.

For more than a quarter of a mile Dick Prescott ran at the best speed that he could summon. Then, after glancing back, he slowed down to a walk, breathing hard. It was fortunate that he knew these forests so well, or he might have been at a loss to find the path leading in the most direct way to Gridley.

Finally he came out on a more traveled road. After keeping along for another half mile or so he heard a horse behind him and the sound of wheels as well.

"I won't take any chance on that," muttered the boy. Bounding over a stone wall he lay low until the vehicle came up. Peering between the stones of the wall Dick made out an unmistakable farmer.

"Hey, there!" cried Dick, leaping up and bounding over the wall. "Give me a ride, please, mister!"

"Well, I swan! Who are ye—dropping from the skies that-a-fashion?" demanded the astounded driver, reining up.

"Grammar School boy from Gridley," Dick replied. "Going that way?"

"I guess I've seen you before," murmured the farmer, as Prescott went closer. "Your pa runs a bookstore, don't he?"

"Yes. Are you going to Gridley?"

"Straight."

"Then please take me."

Not waiting for an answer Dick climbed up to the seat.

"How do you come so far out of the way?" asked the farmer, as he started the horse.

"I'd tell you, but for one thing," Dick laughed.

"What's that, son?"

"You wouldn't believe me."

"Wouldn't believe old Prescott's boy?" demanded the farmer. "Well, I would if the boy is half as square as his dad."

Thus encouraged Dick began to tell his story. Some past events the farmer already knew. This inclined him very strongly to believe Dick's strange tale.

Once in Gridley the farmer drove the Grammar School boy straight to the police station.

"Dick Prescott?" shouted the chief. "Boy, your parents are crazy over your disappearance. What part of the skies did you drop from? And I've four of my men out trying to track you! Tell me what has happened."

"I will if you'll walk around to the store with me," Dick offered, smiling. "But the first thing I'm going to start to do is to show my father and mother that I'm safe."

The farmer good-naturedly offered to drive them both around to the Prescott store. On the way Dick told some of his story. The rest had to wait until he had shown himself to his parents. Then Mr. and Mrs. Prescott heard the story, too.

"This isn't really a case for me," said the chief of police. "It's for the sheriff. I must get him on the 'phone."

The news spread with great rapidity. Dave Darrin, Greg Holmes and all the other chums of Dick & Co. were on hand by the time that Dick had finished a belated supper with splendid appetite.

"May I go out on the street with the fellows?" Dick asked his mother.

"Yes; if you'll keep on the lighted parts of the streets," smiled his mother. "Although I'm not very much afraid of any more trouble overtaking you when you have all your friends with you."

Later that night a party of sheriff's searchers came upon Driggs, not far from the old mill site. The fellow, fearing prompt pursuit, had endeavored to get away, but the pain in his stiffening knee had prevented his going very far. Ab. Dexter had started with his injured confederate, but had finally played the sneak and fled. However, Dexter, too was caught later that night, while endeavoring to board a train two stations away from Gridley.

Mrs. Dexter, of course, was notified as to what had happened.

For this latest outrage against Dick the rascally pair were not tried. This was for the very simple reason that Dick would have furnished the sole evidence for the prosecution, and the law would have required another witness to corroborate young Prescott's testimony.

However, both men were held as fugitives from justice, for having jumped their bail on their original trial. Both were now held without bail and were presently tried before the higher court.

Both were found guilty, of course. As it is the privilege of the court of resort to impose a heavier punishment than the original one appealed from, Dexter and Driggs were both sent to jail for a year—the highest penalty possible under the circumstances.

"That man will bother me worse than ever as soon as he gets out," complained Mrs. Dexter to Dick and Dave one day.

"If he finds you," added Dick, by way of a hint.

"If he finds me? What you mean by that?"

"Mrs. Dexter, you're not obliged to live in Gridley. Why don't you slip away from here, one of these near days, without letting a soul know where you and your little girl are going. With all your money you could go to Europe or to the Pacific Coast. At a great distance from here you can live securely. Dexter will never have any money if he has to earn it. Go a few thousand miles from here, and, even if Dexter found out where you were, he wouldn't be able to reach you. No—don't tell even us where you are going."

Mrs. Dexter followed that very sensible advice. She and Myra vanished completely one day not long after.

Before that good but timid woman went away, however, she did her best to provide some suitable reward for the Grammar School boys who had proved her staunchest friends and protectors, but they refused to consider any reward.

Dexter, when at last at liberty, must have known of his wife's flights to parts unknown, for he never revisited Gridley, and was not again heard of there.

Dick Prescott's last and greatest adventure placed him securely on the pinnacle of local fame. Where, in all the world, was there another Grammar School boy who had been through as much, or shown as much daring?

Even that shrewd and rather dryly spoken judge of boys and girls Old Dut, took the latest happenings as the text for a little address to the members of his class. He wound up by saying:

"In a few months more this present class will have passed on, some going to High School and many more to their life employment. This present class will be gone, and another class here in its place. Yet I believe I can say in all truthfulness that I shall remember this present class always with pride as the class containing the bravest and brightest boys—and the finest girls—of any class that has been graduated from the Central Grammar School."

It is not our purpose, however, to take leave of Dick Prescott and our other young friends. There was too much yet ahead of them—absorbing happenings that merit being recorded in other volumes. We shall meet Dick, Dave, Greg, Tom and all of the chums once more in the next volume, which is published under the title: "The Grammar School Boys Snowbound; Or, Dick & Co. at Winter Sports." Here we shall find them amid stranger and even more thrilling adventures.

THE END